MIST OF THE MORNING

Mist of the Morning

Copyright Jenny Glazebrook, 2015

Published by Jenny Glazebrook

www.jennyglazebrook.com

Gundagai, NSW

Typesetting by Book Whispers (www.bookwhispers.com.au)
Cover design created by Kremena Petrova (k_petrova84, elance).

National Library of Australia Cataloguing-in-Publication entry (pbk)

Author: Glazebrook, Jenny, author.

Title: Mist of the Morning / Jenny Glazebrook.

ISBN: 9780992536367 (paperback)

Series: Glazebrook, Jenny. Aussie sky. 4

Target Audience: For young adults.

Subjects: Man-woman relationships--Fiction.

                 Interpersonal relations--Fiction.

                 Young adult fiction.

Dewey Number: A823.4

MIST OF THE MORNING

Aussie Sky Series

Jenny Glazebrook

Colossian 3:3
'Hidden with Christ in God'

To Nari,

Sometimes I hear about someone who has read my books
and God places His deep love for them in my heart.
I have never met you but I have felt led to pray for you.
For this reason I believe God has a special purpose for you.
May you know His hand in every detail of your life.
May He use you to encourage others,
replacing confusion with clarity
(as He did for Misty in this story)
and bringing Jesus' love to the lost.

Chapter One

Misty never dreamed her life would end this way. It was so wrong. Why couldn't she die doing something heroic like saving somebody's life? Or at least doing something she loved? Why couldn't she have fallen from her horse during a performance? She wanted her life to count for something. She blew out a breath and glared at the monitor beside her bed. The steady pulsating as it measured her brain activity was annoying, but it meant she was still alive. Why couldn't she be normal?

Footsteps sounded down the hall and her heart beat faster. She recognised that stride. And that voice. And the concerned face that peered around the hospital curtain. Blaze had come! She threw herself over the side of the bed and flung her arms around him.

His deep chuckle rumbled in her ear. 'Are patients allowed to perform such acrobatic stunts?'

The fear threatening to overwhelm her rolled away and she felt the full force of the smile that filled her face. 'I don't know, but they can't stop me.'

'I'm sure they can't!' He grinned back before looking down at her cannula. The annoying tube had somehow wound its way around him.

He carefully removed it and her smile dissolved. 'Blaze, did they tell you why I'm here? That I'll probably never perform any kind of stunts again after this surgery? I might never ride a horse again.'

'Yes. Bonnie told me.'

Bonnie. His new wife. Her heart sank further and she lowered herself back onto the bed. 'You shouldn't be here. You should be with her. I don't want you to cut your honeymoon short because of me.'

His dark eyes softened. 'I know, but I had to be here. You're my sister. Bonnie understands.'

'She's not upset?'

'No. She's the one who made me come.'

'How did you know I'm here? Starre promised not to tell.'

He gave a sheepish grin. 'You made Starre promise not to tell me. So she told Bonnie instead.'

She should feel annoyed, but right now she could have hugged Starre. It was so good to have Blaze here. He was studying her as he settled himself into the chair beside her bed.

'I hope you don't mind. I thought you might throw me out, but Bonnie insisted I should come anyway. She said she has a lifetime with me so it doesn't matter if I take a few days to be with you.'

She dimpled at him, letting him know she wasn't upset. 'I think you couldn't have picked a better wife. But God did so much to get you two together. I don't want to come between you.'

He laughed. 'Don't you worry about that. Fire or storm or disease or conflict aren't enough to separate two people if God has planned for them to be together.'

He was right. It was a miracle that Blaze and Bonnie had found each other again after so many years and so much heartache. 'I still can't believe how God brought you two together. Who would have believed what God had planned all along?'

He nodded. 'I know. I thought she was going to die when she was caught in that burning stable. Then I thought I was going to die when I had tetanus.'

She caught her breath as the blood drained from her face. His arm came out to support her. 'Misty?'

'I'm scared, Blaze. But you both survived.'

His eyes widened, 'You think you're going to die?'

She shrugged but felt the sting of tears in her eyes and knew they had betrayed her. She was terrified. Her mother had died. Death was a reality. Everyone presumed her mother died giving birth to the twins, but what if her mother had the same condition she had? The specialist said it was hereditary and was triggered by stress. Her grandmother had it. It was possible her mother had it too. Certainly giving birth could be classed as stressful. Maybe giving birth had triggered it and killed her.

She looked up as Blaze laid a hand on her arm, carefully avoiding the cannula and tube. 'It's going to be okay, Misty. You have the best neurosurgeon in the country. But even if he wasn't the best, we have to remember Colossians 3:3.'

'I know.' She drew in another deep breath. 'Whatever happens it's going to be okay. Whether I live or die, God is with me and will never leave me alone.' She leaned back on the pillows and forced a smile.

He grinned. 'Yes, but I still don't think you're going to die. Not yet. I reckon God likes a good love story. That's part of the reason he spared my life and Bonnie's. And I think that young man waiting for you out in the corridor would like to be part of God's story for your life.'

She blushed as she fought her smile. Then a shadow filled her heart again, settling somewhere deep in her soul. 'Blaze, if I die, tell him I love him.'

His eyes darkened in pain. 'You're not going to die. You tell him.'

'You can't know that. I like your theory about God and love stories, but I don't really think we can depend on it.'

He looked sheepish again. 'Yeah, maybe not. It sounded good though, didn't it?'

'The doctor said brains are complex and he can't guarantee anything.'

Their conversation was cut off as a wardsman breezed into the room. 'Misty Clements?'

She nodded, thinking he was way too cheerful. Clearly he didn't know what was at stake today.

He placed two solid hands on the end of her bed. 'Your turn. Ready to go?'

Ready? She would never be ready. But then Blaze leaned over the bed and gave her a tight hug. 'Colossians 3:3, Misty. Whether you live or die, there's no need to be afraid. I'll be praying every step of the way.'

He was right, so why did she still feel afraid? She couldn't remember feeling fear like this before; apart from one time. As the bed was wheeled along the corridor and she caught her last glimpse of Blaze, her mind filled with memories of that day eighteen months ago; the day she almost lost her brother.

***

Eighteen months earlier …

Misty woke and sat bolt upright. Adrenalin pumped through her but she didn't know why. Her eyes darted across the messy room to Starre's bed. It was empty, so what had woken her with such a start? She heard it again – a loud banging just outside the window. It sounded like someone was pounding on the door of Blaze's caravan.

It reminded her of the days Marcos, the circus ringmaster, would pound on their caravan doors to get them out of bed after a late night performing. But they weren't in the circus anymore and there was no reason to be jarred awake like this. The pounding came again.

'Blaze! Quick! Somethings happened to Peter Pan.'

She jumped out of bed at the sound of Starre's urgent voice. It took a lot to shake Starre but she sounded desperate. The banging began again, more insistent this time. She raced across the clothes covering her floor and came to the window. A sleepy

Blaze opened his caravan door. He shook the dark, tousled hair out of his eyes and blinked a few times.

'Blaze, Peter Pan is really sick. He's shaking and rolling his eyes.'

He was racing out toward the stables in his pyjamas before Starre had finished speaking. Misty followed. She almost ran into the twins, as they also charged outside. Their dark hair poked up in all directions as they threw each other confused looks.

As soon as Misty saw Peter Pan, she knew it was not good. The magnificent horse stood with his head sagging, his whole body quivering. He didn't even look in Blaze's direction when he gently called his name and tried to soothe him.

'What is it?'

He shook his head. 'I have no idea but it's bad.'

As the Clements family waited for the vet, Blaze instructed them to move the other horses from the stable into the paddock.

'Peter Pan could be contagious.' He sounded weary and Misty put a hand on his shoulder. If Victorian Dream were this sick she would be hysterical. In fact she felt a bit that way now. Blaze gave a half-hearted smile before he sat down beside Peter Pan and waited. She sat too, burying her head in Peter Pan's neck and embracing his horsey smell. He was Blaze's horse but she loved him just as much as he did. The other family members were out in the paddock, checking on their own horses, but she couldn't leave Blaze and Peter Pan.

'What will we do if he dies?' She raised her head, her voice coming out in a whisper.

Blaze bit his lip. 'This is nothing, Misty. It's not like we're losing a human, here.'

His earnest dark eyes were searching hers and a lump grew in her throat. None of them would ever forget the day their friend, Bonnie, attempted to rescue their horses from a burning stable and was badly burned in the process. Blaze was right. Losing a horse like Peter Pan would be a tragedy but it would never compare with losing a human life. 'Do you think Bonnie's okay?'

'I don't know but I pray for her just about every day.' He looked pained and she knew it hurt him to think of Bonnie Blake.

'It was strange the way she left without even saying goodbye.'

He only nodded and she knew she should change the subject. He had enough to worry about with his horse so sick.

Peter Pan let out a weak whinny and immediately he was completely focused on his horse, speaking gently, attempting to calm him. She watched and knew that despite his belief that humans were worth more than animals, he would be devastated if Peter Pan died. In fact, she could guarantee he was praying as he closed his eyes, his hand resting gently on the horse's flailing head.

***

'Tetanus,' the vet told them. 'And if I'm honest, I have to say I've never heard of a horse recovering from tetanus, especially when it's so far advanced.'

Blaze nodded resignedly. He spoke with the vet for a few minutes before turning to the triplets and twins who were listening intently.

'Remember, Storm has his exam presentation today.' A worried frown creased his brow. 'And we can't use any of the horses while they're in quarantine.'

Misty's mouth dropped open. In her concern over Peter Pan she had forgotten Storm's gymnastics assessment. It was the whole reason Blaze had come home from Bible college for a few days. Storm's performance included Blaze and Peter Pan. Storm had put his years in the circus to good use and entwined circus moves and acrobatics with his required gymnastics moves. The result was a breathtaking show of athleticism and agility atop his magnificent horse. Now it was out of the question.

She ran a shaky hand through her tangled hair. 'What are we going to do?'

To their surprise it was Beauty who answered. 'We'll do it without the horses, of course.'

'We?' Storm spun to face his sister.

'We. We used to practise back at the circus without the horses, remember? We had a routine we did every day. And when Victorian Dream was sick we didn't use the horses. It all went pretty well, I reckon. Storm can't do it on his own but he can do it with us – without horses.'

Misty glanced from the faces of her triplets, to the twins, then to Blaze. Nobody said anything but she knew it was finalised. They would all help Storm today. All they had to do was practise and perfect a routine within the next two hours before school. But first they needed to get dressed and do their hair. They were an odd bunch standing out in the paddock in their pyjamas, matching heads of dark hair in disarray. No wonder the students at school still treated them like a circus attraction. Almost two years had passed since the day they packed up their circus life and rode through the gates of Everdeen High School to begin a normal life and get an education. She had thought time would help them fit in but now she wondered if she would ever belong.

Once at school, Misty found herself in one of her most awkward situations yet. The assessment team, along with a whole auditorium of staff and students, were waiting for the performance to begin and she was stuck in the toilets. The door had slammed shut behind her and now it refused to budge.

In frustration, she gave it a forceful tug, then gasped as the handle came off in her hand. How was she supposed to open the jammed door now? It was no use banging on it or yelling for someone to come and get her. No one was close enough to hear. They were all waiting for her in the auditorium.

Giving a bemused shake of her head, she attempted to remain calm and think. There was a row of windows high above. She could climb to the top of the toilet seat and force her way through.

But what if there was nothing to lower herself down onto once she was through? Should she make a leap to the ground and hope she didn't break her ankle?

'Keep calm.' She repeated the words she used almost every day of her clumsy, accident-prone life. If only she hadn't chosen to make that typical last minute dash to the toilets before the performance. She hated the toilets. The unfamiliar smell of disinfectant and the stark, clean bareness of the room were as far removed from the familiar smell of horses and her own messy home as you could get.

'Hey Misty, are you in here?'

She breathed a sigh of relief at her sister's voice calling outside the door.

'Starre, can you open the door? It's stuck.'

'I can't. There's no handle.'

She glanced down at the handle still in her hand. 'You'll have to shove from your side.'

A thud came before the door flew open and Starre stood there, panting. 'Quick! We're starting.'

She raced to the auditorium behind her sister and flew up onto the stage. The school cheered at their arrival and she blushed, knowing it was her fault the performance had not begun as smoothly as it should have. It wasn't the first time and she knew it wouldn't be the last.

'Get ready,' Storm growled in annoyance. 'We're starting.'

'I'm ready.' She glared and for a moment he was stunned into silence. Then he pointed to her hand.

'What's that?'

She glanced down to the door handle still in her hand and couldn't help the chuckle that escaped. 'Nothing.'

He watched as she let it drop to the floor and set her eyes on the stage. From this moment, she would not make any more mistakes. Once all eyes were on her, every ounce of strength and concentration would go into presenting a perfect show. No one would guess that only moments before she had been lost and helpless in everyday life.

The triplets and twins watched Blaze closely for his signal to begin.

'I thought Storm was going to do something on his horse,' a student whispered. Misty didn't look. She was focused on Blaze. He gave the signal and one by one the Clements family came onto the stage in a flash of colour and athleticism. Cartwheels were followed by backflips and handstands performed in perfect unison. There was silence as the routine went into full swing. She back-flipped her way to where Prince stood in position beside Blaze, hands bent up at the elbows and palms out. She knew Starre was right beside her doing exactly as she was. With a final flip she stood on her hands before Blaze. He lifted her smoothly by the ankles until she balanced on his hands, high in the air. However, his hands were shaking as though today it was an effort. She wished she could look at his face to check if he was okay but she had to remain completely focused on the twins, who now cartwheeled forward and gave a magnificent leap into the air. A gasp went through the crowd and Misty felt the pressure on her hands as Beauty landed and balanced there, joining hands with Storm, who now balanced on Starre. She always loved the moment when mouths dropped open in awe. She smiled, feeling right at home. Her family had been the star attraction at their circus. Even without their horses they were heart-stopping.

When the performance was finished, she tuned out the applause that erupted through the auditorium, along with the approving nods of the assessors. She was watching Blaze. He was pale and kept rubbing his jaw as though it was hurting. He hadn't eaten any breakfast but then, he was upset about Peter Pan.

'Blaze? Are you okay?'

His dark eyes met hers and what she saw shook her to the core. Fear. The confident, in control Blaze was afraid. He reached a hand back to his jaw, seeming unable to speak.

She moved to his side. 'Do you need to go home?'

He simply nodded. The students were already being directed out of the auditorium. She glanced around for Starre but she had gone. She walked with Blaze out the school gate. If her brother needed her, she would be there for him the way he had always been there for her.

Normally each of the Clements children rode their horses to and from school, but one glance into the paddock beside the school reminded Misty that Blaze's horse was fighting for his life. All the others were stuck at home until they were given the all-clear.

She wondered if Blaze's uncharacteristic illness was due to his concern over Peter Pan. Yet he hardly seemed aware of anything right now. He seemed dazed.

His face suddenly drained of all colour and he gasped.

'Blaze?' She lunged at him as he fell to the ground. His eyes rolled back in his head and he shook uncontrollably. She screamed in terror, then ran back in the school gate. She needed help!

Moments later he was surrounded by a crowd of people carrying out first aid and she heard them say the ambulance was on its way. She watched in frustration and helplessness. If only she could push through this crowd of people surrounding him to see if he was all right.

Chapter Two

Misty sat beside Blaze's hospital bed. She hated this small, white room. She hated the smell and the sounds and she hated that her brother lay so still with tubes coming from his mouth, nose and arms. She wanted to beg him to live, to take away this awful helplessness, but she could do nothing.

He stirred restlessly and immediately she was standing beside him, her hand grasping his. 'Blaze?'

He moaned and his body convulsed once more. He was muttering something and she strained to hear. 'Blaze?'

Starre put a hand on her arm. 'He's still unconscious, Misty.'

She spun to face her sister. 'I have to know what he's saying, Starre!' Tears broke free and ran down her face. 'What's he saying?'

Starre studied her, then pulled her down to the seat beside her. 'He's not making any sense. It's just 'cause he's got such a high fever, the doctor said.'

She shook her head. 'No, he was saying something.'

Starre rubbed a hand across her eyes. 'He's been saying the same thing over and over but it doesn't make sense.'

He began muttering again. Misty's desperate eyes were on Starre.

'Hidden with what?'

'Hidden with Christ. He keeps saying, "Hidden with Christ in God".'

'What's it mean?'

'I have no idea. Probably nothing.'

'But what if he's trying to tell us something?'

Starre sighed. 'Misty, he doesn't even know we're here.'

She didn't want to believe it. She couldn't. But they all kept telling her the same thing – Blaze might never speak again. He might not give her any last support or advice. He might not give her any special message to carry her through the rest of her life. But at least she could speak to him. She could tell him how much he meant to her.

Quietly, as though Starre was not even in the room, she leaned forward. 'You were right, Blaze.' She held in another sob that threatened to break free. His black hair was dark against the white, plastic smelling pillow. 'Horses aren't as important as people.' She touched his limp hand. 'I know that now. I believe in your God because I have to believe you're going to heaven. It's the only comfort I have if something happens to you. But you have to fight, because if you live through this, I will live the rest of my life for God. I will even give Victorian Dream away.'

The words came out all jumbled, as they always did when she was stressed, but Blaze would understand. He always did. All that mattered now was his survival. She watched for signs of life but he didn't move. His breathing sounded weak and shallow, and his body still convulsed occasionally, sending machines into a chorus of beeps.

Dizziness overwhelmed her and for a moment she feared she might faint. She had never imagined her beloved horses could be the death of Blaze. He had caught tetanus too, the doctors said. The same terrifying illness that had finally snuffed out the life of Blaze's horse, Peter Pan only a few hours ago.

'Come on, Misty. We have to get back to school.'

She turned to her sister, shaking the hand from her arm. 'I can't.'

'I know how you feel but we have our final exams. We can't just throw away the last two years of studying. Blaze wouldn't want that.'

It was true but right now there was no way she could concentrate on exams. She didn't want to be here either, watching the life slowly drain from Blaze. She didn't want to be anywhere. She didn't want to exist.

'Come on,' Starre coaxed.

With a final look at Blaze, Misty managed to stand. She waited for her head to stop spinning, then followed her sister from the room. 'He mill wake it!' she declared emphatically, frustrated by the way she mixed up her words.

Her head cleared a bit once they were in the sunshine. She didn't want to go back to that hospital, ever. She walked through the school gate beside Starre, knowing everyone would have heard that Peter Pan had died and that Blaze's life hung in the balance; that at any moment they could receive the tragic news his breathing had stopped. Sympathetic looks were cast their way but few students had anything to say.

Prince raced out to meet them, hope in his eyes. 'It's going to be okay. I've been talking to Rachel Seton and she doesn't believe God will let Blaze die.'

Misty would have laughed had she not been so sad. Rachel Seton was the local minister's daughter and her parents had recently been killed on a mission trip overseas. How could Rachel think Blaze would survive? Weren't Rachel's parents proof that believing in God was no guarantee nothing bad would happen to you?

The exam room was cold and silent as she sat beside Starre and behind Prince. Starre relayed the latest details of Blaze's condition to their triplet, while she tried to remember what exam she was taking. The teacher began a constant stream of instructions and she attempted to untangle the meaning. The more she tried, the more Blaze's words clouded her thinking.

Hidden with Christ in God.

'It has to mean something. I know it does!'

Unthinkingly, she scrawled the words across her note paper, then saw Starre looking over.

'They're just words, Misty. You need to forget about them.'

But she couldn't. This feeling was too strong. 'I have to know!' She absently took the exam paper from the supervisor's hand, glancing from her brother, Prince, back to Starre. Being a triplet had been her security for so long but suddenly it wasn't enough. For the first time in her life, she felt completely alone. She longed to make a life for herself. She couldn't keep depending on the fact that she was a triplet who had come from a circus. What if something happened to Prince and Starre? Then where would she be?

School is not for me. She stared at the words she had scribbled on the exam paper. *I can't even write properly.*

Why had she wasted so much time in school when she knew she would never belong? It was time to go out on her own. She would throw her life into the hands of the God Blaze trusted and see what happened. She had tried to make something of her life and failed miserably, but maybe, just maybe, God could do something with her that was worthwhile. Maybe he could make her like Blaze – caring, respectable, even academic. It was worth a try, anyway. But first, she had to discover the meaning of those words: 'Hidden with Christ in God'.

Although Blaze continued to struggle for his life, the moment Sunday morning dawned, Misty knew it was time to find her own life. Victorian Dream had been cleared of tetanus and she just wanted to ride. None of her family questioned her as she prepared a picnic lunch and set out. They were headed to the hospital and had only Blaze on their minds.

First she wanted to find a church. She needed answers about Blaze's strange words. Through her mind, they tumbled over and over. 'Hidden with Christ in God'.

She also knew that if she was really going to throw her life into God's hands and be a Christian she needed to find out what that meant. But she didn't want to go to Blaze's church where everyone would be asking how he was and giving her pitying looks. She would go to the next town. Then she would spend the rest of the day looking for work on local farms. It would be so good to get a job, to escape school, to become independent, to get Victorian Dream safely away from the paddock where Peter Pan had died, and most of all, to forget about Blaze lying in hospital fighting for his life.

Chapter Three

Roy Haydeen sat outside church, his hazel eyes watchful through the morning mist. No one ever arrived for church this late but his father insisted he should wait at least fifteen minutes just in case. He was as bored inside the church as he was outside, so he might as well stay out a few minutes longer. He scratched a piece of broken brick along the cement path.

Movement caught his eye and he sat up, peering through the rising mist. There, walking across the lawn, ignoring the path, a figure came through the fog. He soon established that he was watching a female with dark, wavy hair that cascaded down her back. Her clothing, however, had him mystified. From what he could make out, she wore a knee length skirt with a crisscross pattern and her floral blouse was too large and looked like it should have been on an old lady.

She stumbled. He prepared to rush to her aid, but to his surprise, she was up again before he could blink and was giving him a sheepish grin. He grinned in response, though he was cautious about what sort of a person he was facing. She had a scar down her left cheek and grazes on her knees. He wondered if she was homeless or had some kind of mental illness.

She stood directly before him, her dark eyes hesitant. It was then it became obvious her delicately flowered blouse was actually inside out.

'I'm looking for the church,' she said. Her voice made him think she was about his age and she sounded quite sane. So what was with the clothing and the stumble? It was almost as though she weren't even real. Maybe he'd wished for her to appear, tired of waiting each Sunday for someone new to come and then being disappointed.

He waved his hand at the building behind him. 'This is the church.'

Her dark eyes widened. 'This?'

He nodded trying not to laugh at her as he ran a hand through his fair hair. Sunday was the only day of the week this habit didn't leave him with dark streaks of dirt through the thick waves.

'So where's the cross? The steeple?'

He chuckled. 'We don't have one. The church is the people, not the building.'

She gave him a quizzical look, then smiled a disarming smile that displayed dimples and perfectly even, white teeth against her browned skin. He had almost expected her to have a tooth missing. He honestly didn't know what to make of this girl or woman, or whatever she was.

She suddenly looked anxious. 'Am I allowed in?'

He nodded. 'Of course. It's already started but there's a few seats left down the back.'

'So why are you out here?'

'I'm on the door. I'm the welcomer today.'

Those dark eyes raised in question. 'Oh?'

He chuckled and held a hand out for her to shake. 'So welcome.'

She held out her own hand and he saw that it was dirty, then felt that it was greasy. He tried not to wipe his hand down his jeans as she gave him a last dimpled smile and walked into the building. He hoped the children in the church wouldn't stare at her the way he had. It was hard not to stare. He wondered about the smell that wafted after her. She smelled like the horses he worked with.

***

17

Misty felt lost behind her dimpled smile and clashing clothes. She had learned to hide her feelings well in her years growing up in the circus and now it was more habit than necessity. This was her first time inside a church and it was as foreign to her as her first day at a public school had been. She looked around, aware of the way she stood out and also aware of the amused looks people gave her as they glanced her way. Once she had enjoyed amusing people but now she longed for respect and something deeper.

Well, it's clear I won't find it here. She made her way to the back of the church and studied the rows of people. There must have been about fifty there and they were all dressed the same, standing the same and speaking the same. She sighed. *Is there no place in the world I can belong?*

The group began to sing the song projected on the front wall and she stared. The words were beyond her understanding. These people were obviously academic, much like her brother, Blaze. Maybe you had to be intelligent to be a Christian.

Despite the need to find out the meaning of her brother's words, she decided to leave. Blaze claimed she would find herself when she found God but she was now doubting God could be found in a church.

With an inward sigh, she turned to leave. But the young man who had stood outside was now sitting at the end of her row, leaving no room to squeeze past. She gazed at his well-built form, sitting so casually in the chair, his long legs stretched out. How could he be so at ease in a place like this? If his legs hadn't stretched so far she would have risked pushing past him but she wasn't likely to get past without tripping or falling into his lap.

She became more restless as each moment passed. *Why did I come? I have to get out of here!* Perspiration began to bead on her forehead and she wiped it away. She was less nervous about a circus performance in front of hundreds of people than she was about sitting here in this building with these religious people.

She had to leave. Silently she stood and studied the path to escape. To her horror, the young man stretched his legs out even further.

Another song was announced and the congregation stood. He stood at a slight angle, blocking her way completely. She shrugged. She would just have to ask him to move.

However, he seemed completely oblivious to her quiet 'excuse me'. She tapped on his solid arm. He didn't budge. She tried again. Surely he had to have felt that? Yet he seemed completely absorbed in the music and sang along heartily.

Desperately, she looked around for another way of escape. The only way was over the back of the chairs but then she would be stuck at the rear of the room with a high wall behind her. However, that wall didn't reach the ceiling and there was a window sill she could climb onto to get up on top of that wall.

Without another moment's thought, she leapt nimbly over the back of the chairs, up to the window sill and onto the top of the wall. The moment she reached the top she could see there were two rooms on the other side and only one had an open door; the one furthest from her. She made her way along the wall until she reached the end, then jumped over the other side.

***

Roy Haydeen was left with his mouth open. It took a few moments to recover and race out the door to see if the girl had survived her leap to the other side of the wall but she was already gone. He just caught a glimpse of her racing across the church lawn and back into the mist. He stood staring after her, feeling as though he were in a dream. Had he imagined the whole thing or had she been real?

Nobody else in the church had witnessed the girl's antics and he hardly knew how to tell them. Telling them would also mean confessing the way he had tried to trap her. His playful prank aimed to ease his boredom seemed childish now he thought about it. Besides, people might suspect he was interested in her and he wasn't willing to admit to that. Instead, he turned to God.

Let me see her again please, Lord. I have to see that girl again!

Chapter Four

Breathing hard, Misty arrived back at the edge of the small town and made her way into a grove of trees. To her relief, Victorian Dream was still tethered there, hidden by an embankment. She was peacefully grazing but looked up and whinnied with delight as Misty reached her. She seemed to understand the distress and confusion in her friend and gently nuzzled her nose into Misty's hair and shoulder.

Misty stroked her. 'There's some things I'll never understand, Dream. I don't get all this God stuff. Maybe it's not for me.'

Yet there was no peace in her explanation. Blaze always insisted God was there, waiting to get her attention and be her closest friend. He wouldn't lie. With a shake of her head, she put her arms around Victorian Dream's neck, wishing she could block out the memories of Blaze lying so ill in the hospital bed.

'You're my best friend, Dream, but you're going to die one day.' Tears welled in her eyes as she buried her head in the horse's neck. 'And if you get tetanus you could even kill me.'

She stepped back and stared at the horse before raising her eyes to heaven. 'I just want Blaze to live, God. That's what I want most of all.' She hesitated, wondering if God would answer her. Blaze said he always did, but she'd never experienced it for herself. She took a deep breath. 'I promise you if you do that, I will live my life for you. Like Blaze does. And if you're listening, I really want a job with horses. I want to be near home, but not too close either. I can't handle school anymore and I need to find who I am without my family. I know I'm asking a lot when I've never really talked to you before, but please let me find a job around here.'

She stepped further back from her horse. It was time to look for a job. God couldn't provide her with one if she didn't look, could he? She headed out of town and toward the local farms, talking to God as she went. 'I just want to feel safe, God. If that's possible in this world ...'

The first farm just outside of town was impressive but there was no sign of horses. She wandered around long enough to establish the fact, then headed back to Victorian Dream. If she wanted to work with horses she would have to look further and it would be much easier on horseback. Rummaging through the picnic bag she had strapped to Victorian Dream, she pulled out her everyday clothes and stood behind the horse as she changed. The church clothes were uncomfortable and slowed her down. Besides, she couldn't bowl up to the door of a farmhouse and ask for work when she was wearing clothes like that. Neither could she ride Victorian Dream very well in a skirt. She shoved her mass of wavy dark hair up under her cap, swung herself up onto Victorian Dream and headed out of town.

The search of the local farms took most of the afternoon. Some farmers stared at her as though she were crazy while others were happy to offer her work. She didn't commit to anything straight away. She wanted to keep her options open and more than anything she wanted to work with horses.

'Please God. If I go much further along this road I'll end up back home in Everdeen.' She stopped. To her left was a dirt road and not far down it was a stone gateway with an arch made of horseshoes. And there in the first paddock were horses. Not just any horses. They were show creatures with unquestionable bloodlines. There were also paddocks with a few head of cattle and sheep.

Her experience lay in horses but she had always been interested in any kind of animal. This place might be perfect.

'Thanks, God.' She rode up the driveway to the main house, hoping the place wasn't as deserted as it appeared.

***

Roy drove down the farm road, tapping out his irritation on the steering wheel. It was late in the afternoon. He glanced at his watch. Five hours! He had been at church a whole five hours! All he wanted to do was go home and process what he had seen that morning. That girl had left his mind reeling but today was their monthly church lunch and it had dragged on and on. It got worse when old Mrs Jerrin started re-telling him the story of her single granddaughter who was looking for a lovely young man to marry. He tried to picture himself marrying a girl who would turn out like Mrs Jerrin one day. No chance.

His attention was drawn to the side of the road. There stood a magnificent horse tethered to one of the trees near the shed. Hadn't the new horse his father planned to buy been a stallion? This horse was no stallion. And why would he have left such a valuable horse out the front?

He stopped short as he caught sight of a figure snooping around the shed. He pulled over and stepped quietly out of the vehicle. He wouldn't risk shutting the door and drawing attention to himself. He crept forward until he saw a fleeting glimpse of the figure disappearing around the back of the shed. With a shout, he gave chase.

Dressed in jeans, a dirty old t-shirt and a cap covering his head, the trespasser began to run. Fury rose within him. Way too much equipment had been stolen lately and he didn't want to lose any more. Worse, what if this person was after the new horse tied out the front?

He soon realised he couldn't catch the trespasser. He had had a head start and was way too fast, despite his slender build. But then he seemed to trip over his own feet and fell down with a cry. He began to rise, but Roy was there within seconds. He knocked him back to the ground, forcing his hands behind his back.

'What are you doing?' He made his voice low and menacing as he growled in the person's ear. The person struggled for all he was worth, his hat falling off in the process. Roy stared at the mass of dark, wavy hair that fell loose. He loosened his grasp. He wasn't dealing with a he, but a she, and the very same one he had met at church this morning.

A question rose in his throat but she had already taken advantage of his surprise and was running again. He watched aghast as she ran straight to the horse tethered to the tree, undid the rope and leapt onto its back with lightning speed. The two raced off together, and Roy was left with his mouth open. She was the best bareback rider he had ever seen.

'Who is she?' he muttered when his voice finally returned. 'What is she doing here?'

***

Misty thanked God for her lucky escape. The farm had seemed deserted until that man appeared from nowhere and scared her with his shout. Her first reaction had been to run but now she wasn't so sure it had been the best idea.

What if that's the farm God had for me? How do I explain why I ran? Now I look like I was doing something wrong.

Was it worth going back and trying again? She remembered the way the horse training equipment had been set up neatly in the shed, surrounded by prize ribbons. Those horses were champion show jumpers. One foal in particular had that same bright response to her that Victorian Dream had. She could tell the foal was strong and intelligent. She wouldn't be able to resist going back. Maybe if she could sneak in again without being seen she could assess whether it was worth asking for a job.

The thought stirred an idea that began to take hold. Marcos, her boss in the circus had been desperate for horses trained by her family. So desperate he had tried to steal them, burning down their stables in the process and leaving Blaze's friend Bonnie badly burned. Marcos would be finished his jail sentence soon and the thought made her nervous. But what if she could give him what he wanted? What if she trained some horses for him? If she could convince these people to sell their horses to Marcos he might finally leave her family alone. She thought about it long into the night.

***

Misty groaned as Starre poked her through the quilt.

'Come on, we've got exams, remember?'

She opened one eye. 'Is it morning already?'

'Yes. Hurry up or we'll be late.'

She buried herself further in her quilt. 'You go. I'm not coming.'

'What? Why not? You're not sick, are you?'

'No.' She searched her mind for an excuse. 'I'm going to spend the day in hospital with Blaze. He needs us. The doctor said he needs to hear our voices, remember?'

Her lie pricked her conscience but she didn't have the energy to explain herself to her family right now. She had no intention of going back into that room where her brother lay fighting for his life. The hospital atmosphere had overwhelmed her last time, leaving her feeling dizzy and confused.

Hidden with Christ, in God. Blaze's words still plagued her as she rode out into the early morning sunshine an hour later. She would need to be more careful today. People were sure to be out and about, working. And she wasn't keen on being crash tackled by that man again.

Excitement mixed with nerves as she arrived at the farm. She tethered Victorian Dream in a much more secluded place this time and began to tiptoe around, every sense on high alert. The horses were truly impressive. A man she guessed to be in his thirties worked with them out in the yard. He was clearly their trainer and handled them with skill.

She itched to work with those horses herself, training and riding them. They had character and spirit. She could tell they were intelligent creatures just by their eyes and response to the quiet words given to them. Still, she needed to know more before she was willing to offer herself as an employee.

Quietly, she made her way to the shed she had almost managed to enter yesterday, before she had been seen. She needed to study the equipment. Knowing what equipment was used would show the quality of care and training the horses were given. She would never work in a place they weren't respected and loved.

All was quiet inside the shed. She crept in. She was studying the bins of horse feed when a soft sound came from behind. She musn't panic. Slowly, carefully, she turned, expecting to see the man who had been training the horses. Instead she found herself facing the young man from church. She began to smile but it died on her lips.

'You again.' His words were quiet but steely. He had her trapped and his narrowed eyes pinned her to the spot. It was then she realised. He must also be the one who wrestled her yesterday. She studied him suspiciously, her heart beating hard in her chest. She had to get out of here. She could see the resolve in his face and knew he would not let her get away this time if he could help it. And he didn't look like he'd be willing to listen to her explanation. He was furious.

'I've done nothing wrong.' She was stammering. Why wouldn't her words come out clearly? He seemed to understand her anyway.

'So why run from me?' He took a step closer. 'All I want to do is ask you a few questions.'

Panic overwhelmed her and she blinked hard, knowing that

in this state she wouldn't be able to make herself understood. Stress always made her words incomprehensible. Her best option was to get out of here and find another place to work.

His expression seemed to soften. 'I think I have a right to know why you're on my farm.'

He didn't think he had a right to know. He knew he did. She moved toward the door but he was there, blocking her way.

'Come on,' he almost pleaded. 'Cooperate.'

She studied him. His whole body was tense as he waited for her next move. He was muscular and solid and there was no way she could fight him. She would have to rely on speed and the element of surprise that had helped her before. Carefully, she glanced around.

'I can see you planning.'

Her eyes flew back to him. His expression confirmed he was as equally amused as he was determined. Well, Misty was tired of being a joke and she wouldn't put up with it. She raced recklessly toward him then dodged to one side. He was ready for her and blocked her way. She head-butted him in the stomach and he groaned but managed to grab her around the waist. She struck out for all she was worth, but he held her fast.

'Settle down,' he commanded gruffly and a little breathlessly.

She fought harder and managed to swing around enough that she faced him. Then she glanced up and what she saw stopped her. His face was pinched with the effort of holding her. But even though strained, he looked kind. Like Blaze. She relaxed in his arms, despite her heart still beating hard.

***

Roy stared down at the girl, wondering what she was up to. He didn't trust her, and although his grip relaxed, he didn't. Still holding her, he looked down into the dark eyes staring at him. 'Ready to talk?'

She just nodded.

'Can I believe that?'

He saw the way she swallowed hard. She nodded again and he released her. She didn't move until he invited her to sit down on an upturned tree stump there in the shed. She sat, while he sat on one across from her.

'So you are …?'

'Misty.'

The word seemed to be an effort. She licked dry lips and he felt sorry for her. She obviously didn't want to share her last name. He would find that out later.

'And you're here because …?'

'I like your horses.' Her words came out a little clearer and her eyes took on a glow.

'I noticed. Why?'

She shrugged. 'I worked in Marcos' Circus. I performed with horses and yours are good.'

He frowned. 'So you're trying to steal them?'

She stood as though about to run again but he was faster.

'Are you trying to steal them?' He had her arm in his iron grip.

Anger and helplessness passed over her face. 'I looked at them!' She shook his arm off and sat down again, resignation in her expression.

Roy did not sit this time. 'Who told you about them?'

She frowned deeper and stuttered before managing to answer. 'No one. I was looking for work.'

'At church?'

She glared but he didn't blink. 'Come on, you have to admit it seems a bit suspicious. Have you been spying on my family?'

Her shoulders slumped in defeat as the anger seemed to drain from her. 'I just had some questions about God. I didn't know you would be there. My brother is very sick and …'

Her voice faltered and pain passed through her eyes. As Roy studied her, he realised her story made sense. Her brother's sickness would mean he couldn't work in the circus anymore.

So she must have been forced to look for other work. And she wanted a church so she could ask God to heal her brother. The whole circus scenario fitted her unusual clothes and the amazing acrobatics he had witnessed from her. An idea began to form in his mind. 'Do you train horses as well as you ride them?'

She nodded but he had to check. 'So you've had experience training and caring for them?'

Again, she nodded. 'I trained Victorian Dream – my horse.'

He smiled. 'Well, I can offer you a job. I think God sent you at just the right time. Charlie, my horse trainer, suggested I find more help for the horses. He spends most of his time taking the horses to shows these days and doesn't have as much time for training.'

Misty studied his face for a moment and he watched, fascinated, as dimples grew deep in her cheeks and her relieved smile revealed those perfect, white teeth.

'You want me to train your horses?'

'I do.'

'Thank you,' she whispered breathlessly. 'I can't thank you enough!'

Roy tried to set Misty at ease as he walked her back to her horse. He didn't make it obvious he was studying her. She was very slim, almost skinny. Bruises marked her arms and she had a scar down one cheek alongside a streak of dirt. Yet she was poised and beautiful. She was unlike anyone he'd ever known.

It crossed his mind that she was escaping some kind of abuse. Something had to explain the bruises. The best thing would be to help her escape if that was the case. Maybe the story about her brother was made up. But no, sincerity had shone from her eyes when she spoke of him. But there was definitely more going on than she had revealed.

'We have a cottage you can stay in while you work here.' He hesitated. 'Will you need your brother to stay with you?'

She shook her head. 'No. He's in hospital. He'll be there for a while.'

'Which hospital?'

'Ederveen.'

Roy smiled. 'You mean Everdeen.' She must be exhausted. His smile disappeared as he realised her jumbled words were more likely a result of the stress she was going through. She was obviously afraid for her brother and lost in the normal world outside the circus. Everything about her was foreign to him; her awkward speech, her appearance and dress, her lifestyle. Even her facial expressions did not allow him to read into her heart and mind the way he wanted to. She had only opened up when she spoke of her sick brother. For a moment he wondered if he had done the right thing, asking God to let him see her again. Maybe she would be more trouble than she was worth. Then again, God must have brought her here for a reason.

***

Misty stared at Roy, wishing she had the courage to ask him the question that most plagued her right now. She wanted to know what Blaze's words meant. 'Hidden with Christ in God'.

Every time he had said it, she wanted to scream at him to say something that made sense. To give her some hope; a way of living without him.

'You'll have to meet my parents,' Roy said in his friendly way, drawing her attention back to the present. 'Dad put the business into my name a few years ago but he still helps out and I still run things by him.'

She simply nodded.

'We also have a couple of other people working with us. You'll have to meet them too.'

He ran his hand through his fair hair, leaving behind dirty streaks, and she smiled. She liked him already. He wasn't likely to judge her for her dirt-streaked face and horsey smelling clothes. This job was perfect. Only a half-hour ride from home and another half-hour ride into town made it far enough from family to be independent but close enough to see them when she needed to. All she needed now was for God to heal Blaze.

Chapter Five

Misty rode quickly toward home. She was excited about her new job and keen to take her few belongings back to the farm cottage. She had no doubt her father would let her do whatever she chose to do. Since Blaze's illness he had become more vague and careless than ever. It was as though he was afraid to take on the responsibility of being the parent he was. Blaze had assumed that responsibility for years now.

She was almost at the house when she slowed. From her horse she could see a familiar figure standing at the door. He knocked a few times, then looked in a window. A sick feeling worked its way from her stomach to her heart. Marcos, the owner of the circus she had worked in, the man who had burned down their old stables, was out of jail.

Her first thought was to hide, but then anger filled her. This man had caused her family too much trouble already. They were going through enough with Blaze in the hospital and the sooner she could send this thief away, the better.

Marcos turned to the sound of Victorian Dream's hoofbeats in the yard. His shifty eyes studied Misty with a wry smile, waiting until she dismounted.

'What are you doing here?' Her voice was cold but she stumbled as she came toward him.

He chuckled, ignoring her question. 'You haven't changed,

have you?'

She glared, offended by his reference to her clumsiness. 'My family can do without you right now.'

He smiled dryly. 'I don't think so, Misty. You see, I'm figuring that now your beloved horses have done this to Blaze you might be more willing to give them up.'

She stared. 'How did you hear about Blaze?'

'I own the best circus in the country. It's my job to know everything. You know that.'

'Leave us alone, Marcos!'

He chuckled in a way that sent shivers down her spine. 'I never leave anything alone until I get my way, little Miss Clements. So what do you say? Do you still want this horse of yours? She could give you tetanus, you know.'

She looked to Victorian Dream. She had told Blaze she would give her horse away but right now she knew she couldn't, not to this man. Marcos could never love Victorian Dream. He saw every creature as a means to make money. He would never change. It was time to put her plan into place. 'What about if I showed you some other horses as good as ours, maybe even better?'

He looked sceptical.

'I've found some.' She licked dry lips. She hated the idea of giving him any horse but what other choice did she have? 'They're show horses and they have character and intelligence. All I have to do is convince the owners to sell them to you.'

His face darkened. 'Sell them? You know I'm not interested in buying. I've already supported your family for years. I'm the reason for your success, you know that. Now you owe me.'

She stared at him and knew there was no way she could convince this evil man to buy. She swallowed hard. She just wanted Marcos out of her life.

'What about ...' she hesitated, while his beady eyes glittered with greed, waiting.

'What about if I let you know where these horses are … and that's it?'

His eyes widened and he smiled a slow, sly smile. 'Now you're thinking like me. But I want more than just a good horse, Misty. I want them trained by the best trainers in the country. That would be you and your family.'

Her heart sank further but she shrugged casually. 'I will train the horses for you. I'll send word when they're ready.'

He grinned a toothy grin and patted her on the shoulder. 'That's my girl. You'd better not let me down.'

She cringed as she backed away from his touch. He came forward again and ran a hand down the scar on her cheek.

'Of course, no one will hear of my name, will they? No one will suspect I have taken the horses.'

She forced herself to stand still and look him in the eye. 'Of course not.'

He gave another chuckle and returned to his car. He waved, then drove close by. 'I'll be back if you don't keep your side of this deal, you know that, don't you?'

She merely nodded, feeling sick to the stomach. What she felt for that man was something akin to hatred, if it wasn't hate itself.

She watched him go, glad no one else in her family had seen him and had to deal with him. That man would do anything to get their horses. Even a previous jail sentence had not stopped him. This time she would get rid of him, once and for all.

***

'What do you mean you're leaving home?' Storm stood, hands on hips, eyes narrowed. She should have waited until the evening meal to tell her siblings, but the moment they arrived home from school she had run out to meet them.

'I have a job. I don't need school anymore.'

Starre looked dismayed. 'Can't you ride from home every day?'

'I could, but it makes much more sense to live there.' She hesitated, thinking how much easier it had been to tell her father. He had listened to her announcement without expression. She had hoped he would reclaim his authority in the family now Blaze couldn't carry it for him, but he didn't seem to care about anything. Not even her leaving.

Storm continued his raging. 'You can't cook. You can't even dress yourself. How do you think you're going to survive?'

For the first time in her life, she didn't feel hurt by her younger brother's heartless, spiteful words, and felt more determined to leave home. He might feel differently if he knew she was doing this for them and that she would get Marcos out of their lives for good.

'What about Blaze?'

That was Starre's quiet, concerned voice and for a moment her heart sank. Then she brightened. 'I'm really not that far away. I'll visit heaps.'

Starre shook her head. 'Soon he might not be there to visit.'

What was she saying? There were tears welling in Starre's expressive dark eyes. 'He's very sick, Misty.'

She shook her head, wondering if life could be worse. She hated the tense atmosphere at home. She hated the grief, the waiting, the wondering. She had to get out of there and start a new life. She had to take action and get rid of Marcos. No longer would she be poor, clumsy Misty who needed the support of her family. She would be pro-active and do something to help.

Her feelings were mixed as she moved into the Haydeen farm cottage and met Roy's parents. Mr Haydeen was much like his son; a fair-haired, smiling, cheerful man with kind eyes. Mrs Haydeen was a little more reserved but Misty liked her. There was something motherly about her and she missed her own mother desperately. Sometimes she would lie in bed at night and remember her mother's smile. Most memories were vague but the smile was always clear and left her with a warm feeling deep inside.

She had only been two when her life was thrown into chaos with the arrival of two tiny, screaming babies and the loss of the calm, loving presence of her mother. She was surrounded by family at home, yet still she felt lonely.

'We're so pleased to have you here.' Mr Haydeen was beaming. 'It will be like having a daughter around. Even things up a bit.'

Mrs Haydeen didn't say anything but she smiled warmly and began wiping the dust off the bed head and side table. She'd even put some flowers in a vase. As Misty set up her belongings in the cottage she wondered if she really could do what she was planning. Could she train the Haydeen's horses, knowing they would be stolen? Could she use this family in such a way? They were being so nice to her.

'I'm doing the right thing,' she told herself, but her heart was questioning. *I am, aren't I, God? I just want to help.*

Chapter Six

Roy didn't know what to make of his new employee. He watched her work with the horses in her quiet, assured way. The horses responded well. He knew she was the best trainer he'd had, and that was saying something. He had seen many horse trainers come and go. He had been helping his father for as long as he could remember. During his school years he'd had to be content to be involved during holidays and after school hours but now he could spend every moment of the day working in the business he loved.

He noticed the way his other employees also watched in silent awe as Misty managed horses they had never been able to handle. At their request, she also performed a few tricks for them, standing on the back of her own cantering horse, then even standing on her hands and smiling around at them with her cheerful, dimpled smile. She had their utmost respect and Roy knew he would have no trouble amongst his employees, as long as the young men didn't take too strong an interest in her. He would keep an eye on the situation and protect her from anyone he needed to.

'Thanks for bringing her here, God,' he found himself praying but the prayer felt awkward. He often prayed in church on Sunday but rarely did he pray throughout the week about his work or everyday life. Now things had changed. The arrival of this intriguing girl was something he couldn't put down to chance.

Misty's second day of work was different from her first. The day before she had felt relaxed and comfortable. Today, she had too much on her mind and it was all to do with the phone call she received from Starre. The doctors said Blaze would have improved by now if he was going to make it. But there had been no change. His words played through her mind again, 'Hidden with Christ in God'. Maybe he had just been delirious and she should try to forget them.

Deep in thought, she walked absently toward the shed. As she entered, her shoulder bumped hard against the frame. She reached to rub it when she caught Roy's gaze. He had seen her misjudge the doorway. Her face flamed at the compassion and concern she saw in his expression. She didn't want to be pitied. She wanted to be respected.

'Everything okay?'

She nodded, then hesitated. 'Not really. I've got a lot on my mind.'

'I can see that. You want some ice for your shoulder?'

'No thanks.'

He just studied her for a moment and she saw the indecision in his eyes.

'It's okay. Really.'

He moved toward her, still looking uncertain. 'Can I help in any way?'

She studied him. His fair hair wasn't quite so out of place today. But then it was still early morning. His jeans were still clean and he looked strong and capable and … well, nice. Like someone she could trust. She took a deep breath. 'Please pray for my brother. He's not improving.'

He nodded. 'I can do that. Have you been praying too?'

She hesitated. 'Kind of.'

He raised one eyebrow but she didn't elaborate. She wasn't sure if trying to make a deal with God was the same as praying. Maybe it wasn't the right thing to tell God she would live for him if he saved her brother's life.

Roy rested a hand on the shoulder she hadn't bumped and the gentle pressure warmed her heart. His concerned kindness was like gentle sunshine on her confused and aching soul.

***

It was three o'clock in the morning when Roy awoke with a start. Misty's brother. He'd forgotten to pray for him but right now his heart was burning with a need to do so. Never had he heard God's voice so clearly. It wasn't that he actually heard words, it was an intense knowledge much stronger than words and it left him both excited and fearful. He knew this was beyond the realm of the natural, and although he believed in God and had committed his life to him as a child, he'd never experienced anything like this before.

He went to his knees and prayed the words on his heart; words that begged for the preservation of the life of a young man he had never met; heartfelt pleas for an extended time on earth to have an impact on other peoples' lives, including Misty's.

Finally, an hour later, he knew his job was done. He allowed himself to fall into bed, rubbing his knees, now indented from the floor. He felt a closeness to God he had never felt before and knew something in his heart had changed.

He woke early in the morning to the sound of the phone ringing. He paused for a moment in silent prayer and wondered at how that supernatural knowledge was still there, a knowledge that this phone call would reveal whether Misty's brother would live or die.

It was Misty's sister, Starre.

'Misty, phone for you.' He knocked on the cottage door, the cordless phone in his hand.

Her face paled as she approached. It was clear she hadn't been up long. Curls poked out in all directions.

'Who is it?' Her slender hand shook as she reached for the phone.

'Your sister.'

He watched as she said hello and sat down at her table. He knew he should leave but he couldn't. He went to her side. It was hard to gather much from her short responses but she appeared upset. When she finally put down the phone, he watched helplessly as she crumpled into a heap and sobbed. What could he do?

Compassion overcame him and he tentatively put an arm around her. To his surprise she threw her arms around him and buried her tear-streaked face in his neck. Though startled, he put both arms around her, something stirring in his heart.

'I'm so sorry, Misty.'

At that, she started and pulled back until those dark eyes were looking earnestly into his.

'No, no, is … it's … it is okay. Blaze is …' She stumbled so badly over her next words that they were incomprehensible.

He frowned, trying to understand, and saw the way her tears started again as she shook her head in frustration.

'Sorry.' Her face flushed with embarrassment. 'Blaze didn't die. I'm just … I …'

She gave up and instead swiped angrily at the tears, unable to look at him. He thought he understood. She was crying with relief. She had been under incredible pressure, expecting her brother to die, and she had held it all in. Now that the danger was past she had set it all free. He began to smile.

'So he's getting better?' He had to make sure he understood.

When she nodded, delight filled him until he felt he would explode. He threw his arms back around her and hugged her tight. 'Thanks, God,' he muttered with rare spontaneity. 'Thank you, God!'

Why he felt so strongly about someone he had never met and why he responded this way to Misty Clements was something he couldn't understand. But he knew God had something to do with it.

Chapter Seven

The improvement in Blaze was miraculous. Family and friends surrounded his bedside, delighted to have him back. He looked tired and weak but he was definitely the same old Blaze. He spoke rationally about the small amount of his sickness he remembered. He admitted that mostly it was all a blur until around three o'clock that morning when it felt like a fog lifted and he re-entered reality.

His dark eyes searched his siblings' and stopped at Prince.

'God is a God of miracles,' he said quietly and a message passed between them. Misty knew Prince didn't believe in God and wondered why Blaze had singled him out. She felt intense frustration at the way he seemed to speak in riddles. He would make comments like that but never explain what they really meant.

It was school time and only she was left there by Blaze's bedside. Roy had insisted she take the day off. Although glad to have time alone with Blaze, she still felt the sense of frustration that so often plagued her.

'What is it?' he asked and she hesitated. He was always discerning. And kind. Like Roy. But Roy spoke in words she could understand. Maybe Blaze thought God was beyond her understanding. Or maybe it was just that he shouldered such a big responsibility, caring for the triplets and twins. He didn't have time to explain things separately to her in simple language. It wasn't his fault she was dense.

'You can say it, Misty.'

She shook her head, tears welling in her eyes. 'Can I really? I don't know if I can. You might not have time to explain or maybe you won't think I'm smart enough.'

He looked hurt and confused. She knew she was being childish and unreasonable. He was alive and awake and all she could do was make accusations. She tried again. 'I'm sick of all the Christian sayings and Bible verses you keep dishing out. I want to understand, but I just don't get them. You keep saying stuff about God but you've never really explained it to me.'

He swallowed hard, trying to sit up against the pillows. 'Explained what, exactly?'

'About how to know God! About how I can be a Christian and be like you. Do you think I can't understand? Is that why you haven't explained it to me?'

'Oh, Misty,' he moaned. 'No.'

Suddenly she was beside him, clutching his hand. 'It's been driving me crazy, Blaze! You kept saying "Hidden with Christ, in God". You have to tell me what it means!'

'I said that when I was delirious?' His eyes widened in wonder.

All the frustration and fears of the last week were building up inside her again and she found herself begging him in desperation. 'You have to tell me what it means. Please!'

He smiled, reaching a hand to hers and she saw the way those tired, dark eyes misted over. In that moment she knew she was important to him. Just as important as Prince.

He squeezed her hand. 'I don't think it's something I can explain easily but I'll try. They are words from the Bible, words that mean a lot to me.'

He reached for the Bible that had been sitting by his bedside from the day he'd been admitted. Prince brought it, insisting Blaze would want it when he woke up.

'Here it is.' He pointed to the words. 'Hidden with Christ in God'.

She didn't bother looking. She hated reading.

'It's a position of complete security. In life or death, whatever happens, I am covered. I'm safe.'

Safe. She had wanted to feel safe for years but the loss of her mother showed how fragile life was. And Marcos being out of jail made her feel constantly on edge.

'How?'

He lay back against the pillows. 'I'll try to explain. We all mess up. None of us are perfect, which puts a barrier between us and God because he is perfect. We're all guilty and God is perfectly just which means we need to pay the price for that. But God's son, Jesus Christ, came and lived a perfect life on our behalf and also died on our behalf to pay for our sin. Now the price is paid and if we accept what Jesus did for us we can know God. Do you understand that?'

She frowned. 'Kind of.'

'Well, I believe that and so I asked him to be my representative to God, if you know what I mean. He's perfect. Because he's my substitute, you could say I am in him. That's the "in Christ" bit. All my mistakes and imperfections are hidden in the fact that Christ took my place.'

She sighed and Blaze squeezed her hand again. 'It's okay, Misty, these things can take years to understand. That's why being a Christian is all about faith. Faith is choosing to trust in God even when you don't understand.'

She smiled ruefully. 'Well, I need to have faith because I don't really understand. It just sounds like a whole lot of words to me.'

'Ask God to help you understand,' he suggested, then smiled. 'Do you want me to try to explain the last bit? The "in God" bit?'

Her eyes brightened. He thought it was worth explaining to her.

'Jesus is God's son so they are part of the one family and they are both eternal, that is, they live forever. Because Jesus is my substitute and I am in him, I am also part of God's family. I am his child and I will also last forever. So even if I had died I would be okay because I am hidden with Christ in God and that's the safest place anybody can ever be. Those words pretty much say that whatever happens I am safe because I am God's and I will be with him forever when I die.'

Misty gave a deep sigh. A deal was a deal and God had kept his side of the agreement. Blaze was alive. 'I believe, Blaze. I don't understand but I'll trust God anyway.'

He took a deep, shaky breath and closed his eyes. 'Then this has all been worth it.' His voice was now weak but his face shone with joy. 'Knowing that you now believe and will get to know God makes it all worth it.'

***

Roy was watching and waiting for Misty to return, even though he had given her the day off. He felt the urge to pray for both Blaze and Misty, and asked God to guide their conversation and give them a special time together.

He was still leaning against the front fence, gazing down the dusty road, when he heard footsteps. He turned to see his father was heading his way. He realised he had probably been out there longer than he realised.

'You seem restless today,' Mr Haydeen commented as he approached.

Roy shuffled uncomfortably. 'I guess I am.'

His father leaned against the fence beside him. 'Everything okay?'

He shrugged, not speaking for a few moments, then turned to his father.

'Dad, have you ever had an experience with God that changed your life? I mean, is he really real to you, because I don't think he was to me until last night. I mean, I believed but I didn't live like I believed. It didn't affect my life. I don't think I've ever heard

42

him speak to me before last night.'

A slow smile formed on his father's weathered face. 'What happened?'

He shrugged. 'I don't even know if I can explain it. I just had to pray. It was like God was right there with me. I felt his presence. And I still can.'

Mr Haydeen nodded and his smile widened. 'Remember the feeling, Roy, because it may not last. God is always here but sometimes he knows we need to feel his presence and be reminded just how real he really is.'

Roy frowned. For a long time he had only treated God as though he was real when it was convenient. But the truth was, God was real and he was always there. He needed to not only believe that in his head, but also in his heart so he could live it day by day. Last night had been a life-changing experience, one he would never forget.

Chapter Eight

Misty rode back to the Haydeen farm. How could Blaze have been dying one day and be so alive the next? It was a miracle and she knew God was the only one she had to thank. She dismounted and allowed Victorian Dream to wander into the paddock and graze in the grass. She was so deep in thought that Roy's voice startled her.

'How'd it go?'

She recovered quickly from her surprise and looked into his kind face. He leaned against the fence rail, looking as though he'd been waiting for her all afternoon. She wished she could explain all that had happened but the words just wouldn't come.

'Good,' she finally managed, frustrated at her own short response. He looked disappointed and she turned away. She truly wanted to connect with him and share her experience but she was emotionally drained and had no energy left to talk.

'I need a sleep,' she tried to explain before heading toward the cottage. He just nodded and watched her go. Her body felt heavy and she struggled to keep her eyes open. Only a few more steps. She pulled open the front door to the cottage, staggered to the bed and collapsed down onto it. Experience told her she wouldn't wake for several hours.

***

Roy wondered what had given him the courage to visit a complete stranger in hospital. Blaze looked weak but managed a warm smile that looked very much like Misty's.

'So you're Roy.'

He nodded. 'Did Misty mention me?'

Blaze's smile widened. 'She did. And I was wishing I could get out of this bed and come to meet you. It seems like God brought you to me instead.' He held out a hand that still bore needle marks from the many days he'd spent in hospital. Roy shook the offered hand, then swallowed hard. Here he was facing a young man his own age who had almost died. He didn't know him, but he had prayed desperately for him. He had so many questions for Blaze. About his sister, about his relationship with God.

'I was praying for you,' he blurted. 'I prayed for ages last night. I've never prayed like that for anyone before.'

Blaze's eyes widened and Roy felt he should explain. 'Misty asked me to. She said she's searching for God but she doesn't quite seem ready to find him yet.'

Blaze took a deep breath. 'She told me.' His dark eyes welled with tears. 'I haven't been very good at sharing Jesus with her. For years I've confused her with trite little sayings and Bible verses, thinking they would help. I never properly explained anything. I made it so complicated when it's really so simple. Did she tell you that?'

Roy shook his head. 'She doesn't even know I'm here.'

'But you are. I believe God brought you into our lives for a good reason. Please help her understand. She needs to understand that God isn't like me.'

'God isn't like me either, Blaze. We all have our weaknesses. But Misty respects you so much. I can tell she does. I don't think she would agree that you have been a bad example.'

Blaze grasped his hand with surprising strength for one who had been so sick. 'Roy, tell her about Jesus! Please! Make sure she gets to know him! I tried to explain today but I still don't know if she understood.'

Roy simply nodded, watching as Blaze lay back and closed his eyes, his energy spent. He had been desperate to ask more about Misty; about her bruises, about the guarded look he often saw in her eyes; about the way she could seem so poised one minute and so absent and clumsy the next. But he knew he needed to leave. First, he did something he had never done before. He sat by Blaze's bed and prayed aloud for both Misty and Blaze. Blaze didn't move and Roy didn't know if he'd even heard the prayer but he knew God had.

He drove home deep in thought, Blaze Clements' earnest, pale face etched in his memory. He was so desperate for his sister to know God. Roy had never taken it all that seriously but this young man had faced death and he knew what mattered. Something stirred within him and he knew he would never be the same again. Through Blaze's testimony he'd had a taste of what it meant to give everything over to God; to rely totally on him, rather than on himself.

***

When Misty awoke from her deep sleep, she felt as though a great load had been lifted. Blaze was going to be okay. She could know God. She didn't have to understand she just had to believe. And she didn't have to struggle through school any more. The only thing that left her uneasy was her deal with Marcos. Even as she went to the horses and began to plan how to train them, she felt no satisfaction. They were magnificent, intelligent creatures and she didn't want to train them for Marcos. She wanted to do it for the Haydeen family.

'But what choice do I have? I'm doing this for my family.'

With that conviction, she forced the uneasiness from her heart and mind and got to work.

Chapter Nine

Misty named the horses she was training. Some already had names but she felt the names didn't do them justice. She took the greatest delight in naming the foal that had caught her attention. He hadn't been named yet, so the name would truly be his.

His mother's name was Connie, not nearly impressive enough for such a creature. But in honour of his mother, she came up with the name Constant Shadow. It fitted him, the way he was at her side like a shadow every moment of the day, taking note of everything she did with the other horses. His bright, intelligent eyes took it all in and she knew he had a heart to learn.

'He's sure taken to you,' Mr Haydeen commented early one morning as he watched her handle the horses, Constant Shadow by her side.

She nodded. 'He's got a lot of potential. He's probably the best horse you've got.'

Mr Haydeen looked surprised. 'Even better than our new thoroughbred stallion?'

She nodded again. 'I reckon. That stallion doesn't have a very good nature. He's too stubborn; likes to do his own thing.'

'I noticed that.'

'Character is good, even thinking for themselves is good, but wanting to go against everything you say or do is a major hassle if you want to train them and work closely with them. You need to be able to trust them.'

Mr Haydeen smiled. 'Roy's right, you know. You're the best trainer we've ever had.'

She blushed at the compliment and went back to her work. She was aware of the respect she was gaining but couldn't enjoy it. How could she, when she was going to betray these people?

It was almost time to knock off work when she looked up to see a familiar figure heading her way. Starre! Her heart leapt with joy and she ran to her sister. 'What are you doing here?'

Starre hugged her tight. 'I've been missing you and I brought you something.'

'I've missed you too. You've got no idea how much!' She stopped. 'What did you bring me?'

Starre reached into her pocket and drew out a mobile phone. 'For you.'

Misty threw her arms around her. It embarrassed her that Roy had to bring the cordless phone from the house whenever there was a phone call for her. Trust Starre to be so thoughtful.

'I've got the number and all the bits and pieces that go with it –' she was cut off as Constant Shadow put his head over her shoulder.

Misty smiled at the admiration she saw in her sister's expression. 'Impressive isn't he?'

Starre nodded. 'Do you think you'd be allowed to show me around?'

'Of course. But how about I get Roy to? I'd like you to meet him.'

The two headed toward the house to find Roy while Misty enjoyed her sister's excitement and enthusiasm over the horses she saw. However, the closer to the house they came, the more she wondered if she was doing the right thing. Starre awed any person who set eyes on her and right now her eyes were sparkling with life. She was poised, beautiful and genuinely good natured. For some reason she didn't like the idea of her sister upstaging her in front of Roy.

Roy was no different from any other male. He stared at Starre and seemed not to know where to put his hands or feet. He shuffled restlessly, and didn't seem to hear what Misty was asking him. Starre did what she did with most males and looked at him with cool, calculated eyes to put him in his place.

'Yeah, yeah, of course I'll show you around.' He glanced at Misty. 'If she's anywhere as good as you, can you convince her to work for me too?'

She threw him a rueful smile. 'Starre's better at everything than I am.' Roy might as well know it now.

'Misty, that's not true.' Starre sounded upset. 'You're like a breath of fresh air. No one can make people smile and laugh like you do.'

She screwed up her nose. 'That's because no one is as clumsy and stupid as me.'

Starre frowned. 'Roy, you're her boss. Make her stop putting herself down.'

He smiled slightly but his gaze held Misty's. 'I will do my best.'

Starre shrugged. 'You'll be doing better than any of the rest of us if you can. Misty's made an art form of putting herself down.'

'I'll see what I can do.' His eyes still held Misty's and there was something deeply admiring and caring about the way he was looking at her. She didn't know what to make of it. He clearly admired Starre but he was also respectful. And his focus seemed to be more on her than her sister. She didn't understand it and she hated the feeling of confusion that overwhelmed her. Starre had clearly noticed and was giving her a meaningful look.

'Okay,' Roy said, pulling on his work boots. 'Let's go and see these horses.'

***

Misty had trouble sleeping that night; a new phenomenon for her. Usually she was so exhausted with the effort of living each day without any major mishaps that she fell asleep the moment her head hit the pillow. Some nights she didn't even make it to the pillow and would wake in the morning with her head at the foot of the bed.

This night, however, her mind was working through the changes that had happened in her life since she had thrown all caution to the wind and given her life to God to see what he would do with it.

I like it, God. She looked up at the ceiling, then changed her gaze. She wasn't sure where to look when she was talking to God. Blaze said he was right there with her, but where exactly? It seemed easier to imagine he was above her than beside her. Maybe that would change as she got to know him better.

I like what you've done with my life, God. Thank you. She sighed. *But please help me to stop making a fool of myself. I hate the way I am so clumsy and can't talk properly when I'm tired or stressed. Please make me smart like Blaze and Starre.*

She lay back on the pillow and attempted to pull up her sheet. She never bothered to make her bed, but somehow the end of the sheet had been tucked under the end of the bed.

'Come on!' She tugged hard. Suddenly it came and her hand clutching the sheet met her cheek bone with force. She let out a cry of pain, feeling her cheek and eye begin to throb. She couldn't help chuckling at herself, though the pain was intense.

Maybe even you can't stop me being clumsy, God. She raced to the freezer to put some ice on her face. When she looked at herself in the mirror she let out an exclamation of dismay. A reddish purple welt was forming and it was not going to be fun trying to explain it to people.

Chapter Ten

'Misty, are you coming to church this morning?'

Roy's voice came through the screen door and she tried to keep out of sight. She screwed up her nose, feeling the tightness in her cheekbone. 'Um, no. I don't think I can.'

She was aware he was trying to catch a glimpse of her and she waved off-handedly toward the door. 'I'll come next week.'

'Come on, come with me today. I'll stick by you.'

She didn't understand why he so badly wanted her to come but it warmed her heart. She almost gave in but caught another glimpse of herself in the mirror. The purple bruise around her eye would make everyone stare and worry. She didn't want to be noticed, let alone pitied.

'Come on, don't be chicken.'

She held her ground. 'I just need to rest today. I'll come to church next week. I promise.'

Through the curtains she saw his shadow hesitate then shrug before heading away. She couldn't hide her eye forever but at least she now had a bit more time.

She managed to hide away all Sunday but when Monday morning came she had to go to work. It would be impossible to avoid people all day but she would try her best. It wasn't long before Roy came in to wish her good morning and see how the training was going. She managed to respond to him while keeping her face averted, focusing instead on the horse she was working with.

'I wondered if something had happened to you.'

She tried to chuckle lightheartedly. 'Nah, I'm fine.'

'I wish you could have come to church.' His footsteps sounded closer while she simply nodded and turned her face evasively.

'Is everything okay?'

He was trying to see her face. 'Yeah, I'm just concentrating.'

He clearly wasn't convinced and stepped directly in front of her. His eyes showed his shock. 'What happened to you?'

She touched a hand to her swollen cheek and black eye. 'I was pulling up my sheet and my hand slipped.'

His expression said he clearly didn't believe her but she didn't bother to reassure him. There was no other explanation to give, so he would just have to live with it.

'Misty?'

'It's true, Roy. That's what happened.' She tried to move away, hiding behind her dark hair as much as she could.

'Promise me? No one assaulted you?' He was now in step beside her.

That's what he thought? She lost focus for a moment and tripped. His hand came out to steady her and flustered, she found herself staring into his eyes. She managed to swallow. 'I promise.'

His eyes searched hers until he seemed satisfied she was telling the truth. 'There's something else I need to know.'

Panic filled her, but she managed to hold his gaze. 'What's that?' Surely he didn't know she was training the horses for Marcos? He must realise she was using different techniques from most show trainers but could he have guessed?

Dizziness overtook her for a moment and she took a deep breath and closed her eyes. When she opened them again he was giving her a strange, almost knowing look.

'I want to know why you do this.'

'Do what?'

'This clumsy business.'

Her eyes widened as she realised what he was suggesting. Anger built up inside her and she gritted her teeth. 'I don't do it on purpose. Why would I?'

He shrugged. 'I don't know. Attention seeking? To get out of doing what you don't want to do, to avoid answering questions you don't want to answer?'

She felt as hurt as she did angry. She had begun to like Roy; to trust him. Now she discovered he thought she was a fake. Without another word she stormed away. The arrogance of him to make such a presumption! As if anyone would make a fool of themselves on purpose. She hated the attention it drew to her, as negative as it was. She'd learned to turn it into a positive by laughing at herself and encouraging others to laugh with her but it was hard work. She would do anything to have 'the curse', as Marcos called it, taken away.

'Misty!' Roy called after her, and there was regret and apology in his tone. 'I was just asking.'

'Well, I don't like the way you asked,' she threw back over her shoulder, fighting the sting of tears at the back of her eyes.

'I'm sorry, okay. Please stop.'

She slowed, then stopped. He caught up with her and ran a hand through his hair, looking uncertain. 'Can I ask a different way?'

She shrugged, then nodded when she saw his genuine regret.

'I guess what I want to understand is how you can be so amazingly nimble on the back of a galloping horse but can't even walk a few metres without bumping into something or tripping over your own feet.'

It was a fair question but she didn't know if she could explain. However, with his sincere, kind eyes looking at her like that she knew she needed to try. 'When I'm on a horse I'm concentrating the whole time. It uses everything I have. I've practised it for years and years. But I can't concentrate like that all the time. I get too tired. I can't concentrate like that when I'm walking or talking. I know everyone else can but I can't. I've just always been that way.'

He seemed to accept her answer and his arm came around her in a quick hug. 'I really am sorry for what I said. Thanks for talking to me.'

She managed to grin up at him. 'We can talk longer if you like but don't forget you're paying me.'

His eyes crinkled in the corners as he smiled. 'In that case, you'd better get back to work.'

She was surprised when he continued to walk by her side to the horses. She forced herself to put his presence out of her mind as she worked. He didn't say much but he was there quietly watching and helping. At first she wondered if she was being assessed but he didn't seem to be questioning anything she was doing and made it clear he didn't doubt her ability. Then she began to wonder if he did suspect something about Marcos. Had he noticed that Constant Shadow and the other foals around the same age were being trained a bit differently and more intensely? Could he tell she was preparing them for circus life?

***

Roy watched Misty work, curious and concerned. He didn't understand why he was so drawn to her. Blaze had begged him to help her understand about Jesus. Well, he was only just beginning to understand it all himself but he knew it was important. He also wanted to know more about this fascinating new employee God had brought into his life.

She turned for a moment and he saw her black eye again. His heart constricted. He didn't like to see her hurt but he now understood why she didn't want to be seen at church. 'So you'll come to church next Sunday, then?'

She had seemed tense all morning but at his question she relaxed and grinned at him, eyes playful. 'If you promise to let me leave if I want to.'

His eyes widened. She must have known he deliberately trapped her in the row at church. But then, she was obviously bright and observant, and she now knew he wasn't deaf or stupid despite pretending to be that Sunday.

'Why would you want to leave?'

She shrugged. 'I don't know. It's all a bit … different. I like being outside. And I don't know when I'm supposed to stand or sing or pray or whatever.'

He was surprised. He hadn't thought about church from an outsider's point of view. He had gone to church almost every Sunday since the day he was born and he felt at home in that environment. He grinned, feeling sheepish. 'I promise to let you leave if you want to.'

She nodded. 'I'll come, then.'

He continued watching her work, fascinated by the way her dimples showed even when she wasn't smiling and wondering why he couldn't bring himself to talk to her more about God. Maybe he was like Blaze, worried he wasn't a good example of what a Christian should be. Until he met Misty he hardly prayed at all unless he was asked to lead the prayer time in church. He also never read his Bible from Sunday to Sunday. It was always there with him at church, almost like a part of his Sunday dress. Sunday was usually the only day he left behind his work clothes and dressed up a little.

For a moment he wondered why he dressed up for church. He studied Misty, now in ripped work jeans and an old t-shirt and remembered the first day he'd seen her, when she'd obviously attempted to dress up a little bit. She'd done a poor job of it but why did she felt she had to? Was church not welcoming and accepting of everyone the way it claimed to be? It was a thought that bothered him and he planned to speak to his father about it.

Chapter Eleven

Misty was pleased with the phone Starre had bought her. It meant Roy had no reason to come to her door which meant he wouldn't see the mess. Tidiness had never been her strong point and it was something she didn't have the energy or inclination to change. When she did tidy up, she was sure to trip over or spill something and make it messy again anyway.

She had passed her new phone number on and so was surprised when Roy once more came down to the cottage holding the cordless phone.

'Some guy for you, Misty.'

Her brow rose in surprise but she took the phone. Roy normally sat and waited for her to finish phone calls but today he seemed keen to disappear. She wondered if he thought the 'some guy' was a boyfriend.

'Hello?'

'My little Misty …'

'Marcos.' Her voice went icy. 'What are you ringing here for?'

'Just to check on progress. How are things?'

She glared into the receiver. 'How did you find me?'

He laughed his unpleasant laugh. 'I asked a question first.'

Shaking her head in frustration, she knew she could not beat someone like Marcos. He was too used to having his own way.

'The horses are doing well.' She tried to stamp down her fury.

She hated the fact that she was training Constant Shadow to go to a man like Marcos. The whole deal was unsettling but she was doing it to ensure the safety of her family. She also knew Roy Haydeen and his family were not wanting for money. Having a few horses stolen would be a setback but not a real problem financially.

'I thought I'd come and give them a check over,' Marcos said.

Her heart went cold. 'No need to do that.'

'I think there is.' There was steel in his voice. 'Your family have tried to trick me before, remember? And we don't want another little stable fire or anything, do we? It would be sad if something happened to Blaze now that he's recovering so well. I'll be there Sunday morning and I expect you to be too.'

It was a threat and an order and Misty knew it wasn't worth fighting. She would never win. 'All right. See you then.'

He chuckled delightedly. 'I'm looking forward to it. You're a good girl, Misty Clements.'

She hung up the phone, feeling sick. She wasn't a good girl. She was about to surrender to the constant manipulations and demands of Marcos, the most deceitful man she had ever met; the man who had so often ridiculed her as a child and made her life a misery. Yet if she could end it all once and for all it would be worth whatever it cost her conscience.

Her mind tumbled over and over as she tried to work out what to tell Roy. She had promised she would go to church with him in the morning but now she couldn't. She had to be there when Marcos arrived. Starre was staying the night and now she would have to get her away from the farm before Marcos arrived. Starre couldn't find out about this!

She swallowed hard and found her throat hurt. Stress often had that effect on her, but this was something more. She glanced around, wishing she had some tissues. She desperately needed to wipe her nose. In the end, she used her sleeve, frustration rising. Surely she wasn't coming down with something? She had enough to deal with already!

'So what do you think of Roy?' Starre asked teasingly as she prepared the evening meal. Starre was used to her untidy ways and had already cleaned out the fridge.

She shrugged, trying to swallow away her sore throat. 'He's my boss.'

Starre smiled. 'Come on, Misty, you can tell me.'

She made herself focus as she met Starre's playful, meaningful look. Suddenly she couldn't think. She didn't even try to talk, knowing her words would come out jumbled. Starre's smile turned to concern. 'You're not feeling well, are you?'

She shook her head miserably, grateful that Starre knew her well enough to recognise the signs and leave her alone. She knew Starre presumed she was confused by her feelings for Roy, never guessing Marcos was the true reason behind the panic rising into a knot in her heart and throat.

***

When Roy knocked on the door that evening, Misty was already fast asleep. Starre sat alone in the kitchen, reading. She looked up and put her book face down on the table and he waited for the cold glare she usually gave him. To his surprise, she smiled.

'Oh, good, it's you. Misty asked me to let you know she's not up to church in the morning. She thinks she's coming down with a cold.'

His heart sank. What excuse was Misty going to come up with next?

'I think it's true.' Starre looked indignant and he realised he must have let his scepticism show. She lifted her chin and glared. 'She's not herself today.'

He nodded, trying not to grin at the perfect show Starre was giving him. He hadn't yet worked out why she wanted to keep him at such a distance. He glanced toward the bed in the room where Misty lay. She was really out to it.

He was about to leave when Starre stopped him. 'Roy, Misty

is … she's different.' Her eyes softened. 'But she's special too. In a good way.'

He nodded. 'I've noticed.'

He waited, hoping Starre would say more, but she didn't. She stuck her nose back into her book. With a quiet goodbye, he turned and left. If he couldn't get Misty to church he would have to think of another way to help her understand about God. Maybe the minister wasn't the one who needed to teach her about God. Maybe he was.

For the first time, Roy watched the church service through an outsider's eyes. He could see how it could be frightening and uncomfortable. His mind began to work on how the church could bring the message of Jesus outside the church building and into the world where most people were comfortable.

'Puppet shows in the park,' he finally resolved. 'I could get together a team of people to learn to do puppets and we can do shows in the park for kids on weekends. Then the parents can hear the message in a clear, simple way as well. It won't be threatening and it'll be fun.'

Pleased with himself, he looked forward to putting his idea to the church. He wanted to get it going as soon as possible.

***

Misty was on edge as she said goodbye to Starre.

'It's okay,' Starre tried to reassure her, misunderstanding the reason for her edginess. 'Roy seemed to understand when I told him you were too sick for church.' She gave a mischievous grin. 'I don't think he's going to stop liking you because you missed church. He'd probably be more upset if you gave him your cold.'

She just nodded and handed Starre the reins to her horse wishing she would leave. Marcos could arrive at any moment.

But Starre hesitated again. 'You sure you don't want me to stay? You're really not well …'

'No. I don't want you to get sick. I want you to go.'

Starre looked unsure but left, while she watched, making sure she didn't change her mind and turn around. Finally Starre was out of sight. Her heart was beating too fast and she felt as though she hadn't slept at all.

'Help me, God,' she whispered, wondering why God felt so far away. It was almost as though God was involved in every part of her life except this part. And yet she could see no other way out. It seemed the best option.

Marcos arrived on time, as eager as a small boy. He marveled over Constant Shadow and greedily eyed off the stallion as well.

'He won't do you any good,' Misty said, longing to go back to the cottage and lie down. 'He's stubborn. I could train him but he would hate it.'

Marcos frowned. 'I don't care if he hates it. I want the best.'

'Well, he's not the best. A horse that hates performing won't perform very well.'

He frowned harder. 'Pity. He looks good.'

She nodded in agreement, wishing he would leave. She had given him her word but clearly a man as dishonest as Marcos didn't feel he could trust anyone else, either.

'So these three will be ready for me in around six months?' He let his eye roam over the fast growing foals.

She nodded. 'Something like that. Like I said, I'll let you know when they're ready.'

There was something in Marcos' expression that scared her. 'Make sure you do.' He gave a leering grin. 'I hear Blaze is improving every day. How lovely for you all.'

She merely nodded, hearing the threat behind his words. She wanted to be left alone. She wanted to feel safe. He looked hard at her. 'You don't seem in top form, though.'

She didn't bother to answer. She needed to wipe her runny nose. Marcos was still studying the horses and eyeing off the equipment in the shed while she glanced around. All she could see was Roy's shirt hanging over the fence where he had left it the day before. Quickly she pulled it off the fence. She needed a tissue and this would have to do.

She watched with relief as Marcos finally started to leave, seeming satisfied with what he had seen. He grinned at her wiping her nose on the shirt.

'You never change, do you?' His laugh was mocking. 'I hope you wash that before you give it back to the poor bloke who owns it.'

She didn't bother to answer as she saw him out the gate then went straight back to the cottage to lie down. She threw the shirt on the floor, vowing she would buy some tissues as soon as she could. She would also wash Roy's shirt and put it back on the fence before he noticed it was missing.

Chapter Twelve

Misty sniffed miserably as she lay on her bed staring at the mess around her. Perhaps if she'd been sick more often in her life she would have made an effort to be tidy. But she was usually outside in the bright, fresh air. She didn't even have the energy to go outside today. This cold seemed to have taken a hold of her.

'Misty, is there anything I can get for you? Roy said you're not feeling too well.' Mrs Haydeen's friendly voice came through the door.

She managed to get up. 'I need some tissues or hankies.' Her throat hurt and she hung her head.

'What about washing? Meals? Anything else?' She glanced around at the clothes strewn across her floor and thought about the small amount of food in her fridge, consisting mostly of a loaf of bread starting to go mouldy. She hadn't done a load of washing since she arrived at the farm but she wasn't about to confess that to Mrs Haydeen. As soon as she was better she would work out how to use the machine in her laundry.

'I wouldn't mind some fruit,' she admitted. 'Hang on, I'll grab you some money.'

Mrs Haydeen shook her head. 'No, it's fine. Roy said he'd cover it.'

'Oh. Okay.' She tried to read into Mrs Haydeen's expression. Did she mind that her son was going out of his way for her? If she did, she didn't show it. Misty wasn't used to people being so kind to her and it was unnerving. Of course, Blaze was always kind, but Blaze was her brother. These people weren't connected to her in any way. It would be easier if they treated her like any other employee. It would make it so much easier to let Marcos steal their horses.

***

After a week of waiting for Misty to improve, Roy could no longer sit back and let his mother talk to her through the screen door.

'She doesn't want anything and she won't let me take her to a doctor,' Mrs Haydeen insisted while he fussed and worried. 'With that cough she's got I think she should go, though.'

He felt helpless. 'Maybe I should call her sister.'

Mrs Haydeen laughed. 'I have. Starre said circus people don't go to doctors. They just get better on their own.'

He shook his head. 'Blaze didn't though, did he? He nearly died.' He paced the floor for a minute more, then turned to his mother. 'I'm going to make her see a doctor. I'm her boss. I can make her go.'

Mrs Haydeen's eyes twinkled. 'I'm interested to see how that turns out.'

***

Misty's week in bed had not been too miserable. Life always seemed full of action and pressure but sickness gave her an excuse to recover from the busyness of life and just think. It also gave her a chance to talk to God. She found it much more satisfying than talking to Victorian Dream. The horse had no power to do anything and couldn't really understand her, but God understood and could do anything, so Blaze said, anyway. She remembered him claiming that God always heard and answered. Sometimes he didn't seem to answer because he was saying 'wait' or 'no', but he always listened and responded.

63

The only thing she couldn't bring herself to talk to God about was Marcos. This was the one area of her life she needed to handle herself. She had felt helpless at the hands of the harsh circus owner for years but now she was doing something about it.

She heard Roy on the cottage verandah. His steps were much more energetic than Mrs Haydeen's familiar, even ones.

'Misty?' He looked through her door. His mouth twitched as she approached and his eyes twinkled. 'What attacked you?'

She put a hand to her head in confusion and realised what he found amusing. She tried to push her hair into some semblance of order.

'My hair likes being messy.' Her voice came out in a raspy croak.

He looked past her and she knew he couldn't have missed the rubbish and clothes lying across her floor. 'Hmm, your hair reminds me of someone.'

She pulled a face at him, still trying to tame her wayward hair.

'Can I come in?'

She opened the door.

Roy looked around and shook his head. 'Seriously, is this how you live? Or is it just because you're sick?'

She coughed a chesty cough. 'I'm not that sick.' She fell weakly into a chair beside him.

He laughed at her declaration, then stared at the shirt lying on the floor. 'I wondered where that got to.'

She followed his gaze and felt heat rise into her cheeks. That shirt! In her sickness she had completely forgotten about it. 'I was going to wash it and give it back.'

He studied her red face. 'You borrowed it?'

'Kind of.'

He shrugged. 'I'll take it. I can wash it.' He reached for it, but she made a grab at it first.

'No, I'll do it. I promise.'

He smiled and shook his head. 'Misty, it's been missing for a week. How long until you actually get to washing it?'

'I'll do it. I will.'

He grinned at her discomfort and reached for it again. 'No, now I want to see what the issue is. What did you spill on it?'

She jumped back, still holding the shirt. 'Nothing.'

He held out his hand. 'Then show it to me.'

She would have to tell him. 'I blew my nose on it, okay?' She knew she sounded defensive and felt the fire in her face. 'I was out in the yard … and well, your shirt was on the fence.'

His expression was incredulous. 'You blew your nose on my shirt?'

'I was desperate. I needed to.'

She was cut off by his laughter ringing through the cottage. 'You're unbelievable, you know that?' He reached forward and grabbed the shirt. 'And I'm not worried by whatever is on the shirt. Let me wash it so I can wear it again.' Teasingly, he began searching the shirt for the evidence.

'Roy,' she pleaded.

He stopped his search. 'Okay, okay. It's not that big an issue though, Misty. Honestly, I don't care.'

She looked at him in disbelief, then slowly let out a sigh of relief. He meant it. He really didn't care. He seemed more amused than anything else. She went to speak but was overtaken by another coughing fit. Finally she stopped, exhausted, eyes streaming.

He had not taken his eyes off her and he now leaned forward. 'I want you to see a doctor. I've made an appointment for this afternoon.'

Her eyes widened and her heart beat hard in her chest.

'I'll come with you.'

She wasn't reassured. Apparently a doctor had come when Beauty and Storm were born but her mother had died. Blaze had been put into hospital under a doctor's care and had nearly died.

Doctors were for the dying. She had never been to see a doctor before. She raised her chin. 'I don't want to go.'

Roy sat taller and his tone was full of authority. 'Misty, you need antibiotics to help you get better. I'm taking you in, so be ready at three o'clock.'

'Anbi what?'

His eyes softened. 'Antibiotics. Medicine.'

She shrugged in defeat. If it was just medicine she was going for, she could cope with that.

She began to cough again and Roy went to the small kitchen. She watched as he picked up the glass she had dropped and cracked. He then picked up another dirty glass. He glanced at it, rinsed it out, filled it and brought it to her.

'Do you know how to use the washing machine?' he suddenly asked.

Her look was sheepish and gave him the answer he needed. He began bundling clothes from the floor into his arms.

'I'm going to put a load on to wash now and as soon as you're better. I'll get Mum to show you how to use it.'

She simply nodded. She didn't have the energy to fight him right now. She wondered what he must think of her. He had clearly been horrified by the state of the cottage and for the first time in her life, being messy bothered her.

Chapter Thirteen

'I've been talking to Mum about you,' Roy admitted candidly as he drove the tired but relieved Misty home. The doctor hadn't been nearly as bad as she had imagined and all she had to do was take antibiotics and rest. 'We'd like you to eat meals with us from now on.'

'But –' Her coughing fit interrupted her and Roy grinned over at her.

'See? No buts allowed.' He returned his eyes to the road.

'That's not part of the employment conditions, though.'

'It is now. It won't cost us that much extra to feed you, and you deserve more than I pay you, anyway.'

Deserve. Her heart sank. She didn't deserve anything from this family.

'So we'll see you at dinner tonight.'

She rested her head back against the seat and closed her eyes. She didn't have the energy to argue but Roy might change his mind once he saw her table manners, or lack of them, and once he had to replace broken plates and glasses. He didn't know what he was getting himself in for.

Apart from continual coughing fits, Misty felt uncomfortable at the Haydeen table. A clean table cloth lay across the table with cutlery neatly arranged, a glass directly above each knife, and a small vase of flowers in the middle beside a salt and pepper shaker. A knife and spoon were to her right, and a large and small fork to her left. She had no idea why she would want two forks but wasn't game to voice her question. Instead, she watched nervously as Mr Haydeen offered to say grace. Each family member held out their hands and she found hers captured in one of Roy's and one of Mrs Haydeen's. She listened as Mr Haydeen thanked God for the food but wondered at how aware she was of Roy's hand holding hers. She wasn't game to look at him but enjoyed the warmth and security she felt while his large, work roughened hand encompassed hers.

She knew it wouldn't take long for her to break something and her glass was the first thing. She somehow managed to knock it onto the floor and apologised profusely while Mr Haydeen picked up the pieces and Mrs Haydeen mopped up the liquid from where it was now running under the table.

'Don't worry about it.' Roy went into the kitchen. He came back holding a plastic cup which he placed in front of her with a playful grin. 'This used to be mine. I used it until I was big enough not to spill things.'

She laughed along with the Haydeens despite her embarrassment. She didn't want Roy to know what she was really like. She liked him and craved his respect. What if he mocked and humiliated her like Marcos had?

She arrived early the next night, hoping to have time to study the table and remember what was used for what.

Mrs Haydeen greeted her with a smile. 'I'm so glad you came early. I haven't had a chance to set the table. Can you get started for me? Cutlery is in this drawer and glasses are in that cupboard.'

Misty's jaw tensed. Her plan had completely backfired. *Come on, it's a simple task,* she chastised herself as she took down some glasses. But her mind had gone blank. Did the glass go above the knife or the larger fork? And which of the forks went on the inside?

'Misty! You're here early.'

She turned at Roy's cheerful greeting and felt her arm go weak as the glass she was holding slipped from her fingers. It landed with a loud crash. She gave a sheepish grin but stopped when Roy didn't return it. He was frowning, no amusement behind those usually kind eyes. He met her gaze then quickly looked away. Something hurt inside. It was as she had feared; he had lost all respect for her now he knew just how clumsy she was. Or worse, did he think she was doing it on purpose to gain his attention?

Mrs Haydeen gave her the reassuring smile she needed, then took over the table setting. She laughed good-naturedly when Mrs Haydeen placed Roy's plastic cup in front of her again, but it bothered her. She should have argued more profusely with him when he insisted she eat with his family.

***

Roy was worried. Only the night before his father had mentioned his concern over Misty's apparent ability to fall asleep anywhere, anytime, and the way she was constantly losing control of her muscles.

'Maybe I'm worrying about nothing but there are some disorders that can cause things like that,' he told Roy.

'Like what?'

'Sleep apnoea or a brain disorder like narcolepsy. Or ...' he hesitated.

'Or what?' Roy pressed, though he knew what his father was thinking.

'Brain tumour.'

Brain tumour. He didn't even want to think about it. In fact, he'd put it out of his mind, telling himself Misty was purely clumsy. But he'd been watching her when she dropped that glass and his father was right. It wasn't as though she had bumped into something that caused her to drop the glass. It was simply as though her hand had stopped holding it. Her whole arm had gone limp for a few brief seconds before she pulled herself together again.

Lord, he prayed, *please don't let it be!*

69

Chapter Fourteen

'You seriously eat at their table every night?' Starre was grinning as she dumped her bag of clothes on the spare bed in the cottage. 'Are you sure you're just an employee?'

'Don't laugh, Starre. You'll be eating with them for the weekend too.'

Starre didn't look worried. She glanced around. 'And it looks like you're having a go at being tidy too. Did Roy teach you to use the washing machine?'

Misty frowned, wondering what Starre found so amusing. 'Actually, no. Mrs Haydeen did.' Starre didn't need to know Roy asked his mother to show her.

Starre smiled as she sat down at the table. 'Well, the tidy bug sure has bitten you. Or is it something else?'

'Like what?' She knew what it was and a heaviness sank down from her shoulders to her heart. It was shame and a feeling of inadequacy. Tidiness had never mattered in the circus and appearance didn't matter unless you were in the ring, performing. It seemed that in normal life you had to be performing every minute of every day, being what everyone else expected you to be.

She felt Starre's arm come around her. 'Hey, I was just teasing, Misty. Honestly, we all love you just the way you are. Including Roy. Especially Roy.'

She managed to smile, but she was troubled. He wouldn't even want to look at her if he knew what she was planning for his horses.

It was even harder to eat at the Haydeen table with Starre there. Starre found her table manners without any problem and was her usual poised, beautiful self. It was clear the Haydeens were taken with her and Misty felt clumsy, dirty and unattractive. She felt even worse when she knocked her dirty fork into her lap, leaving remnants of food on her shirt. Roy brought her a serviette to clean it up. She couldn't return the friendly grin he threw in her direction; she was too busy remembering the admiring way he had watched and listened to Starre speak about her acceptance into uni. Starre had always been bright and nobody ever felt they needed to give her a plastic cup or plate.

She stood to leave as soon as the meal finished but Roy reached for her arm. 'Hey, why not hang around for a bit? There's no work tomorrow.'

She looked to Starre, unsure. He had never invited her to stay after a meal before. He obviously wanted to spend more time with Starre. She couldn't blame him, but it hurt.

***

Roy waited, hoping she would agree to stay. Starre's presence would make it easier to direct his attention somewhere other than Misty. He didn't want to appear infatuated with the dimpled, dark haired girl but he knew he was falling for her. He was also concerned for her health and most nights making sure she had enough sleep was more important than spending more time with her. She was finally coughing less and her energy was returning, but there was still the awful question his father had put in his mind. Was it possible she had a serious illness or disorder?

Starre's eyes sparkled. 'Of course we'll stay. Come on, Misty.'

He led the way into the lounge room before she could argue and pointed to the lounge.

'Have a seat.' He sat opposite and leaned back, his arms

behind his head. 'So how about a game of something?'

'A game?' Misty looked panicked and sat back against the lounge as though trying to get as far away from the suggestion as she could. 'I'm no, I don't, I will, no thanks.'

He grinned. 'I take it that was a no?' He glanced at Starre who gave the slightest nod toward Misty.

'We don't really know any games and I think we're a bit tired.'

By 'we' she clearly meant Misty. Roy wasn't put off. 'Well, tell me about your life in the circus, then. What was it like?'

He hoped Misty would answer but Starre spoke first.

'We were born there. Mum and Dad met in the circus. Mum used to be an Olympic gymnast before she joined the circus and Dad was born in the circus like we were. Dad doesn't perform, he just cares for the horses, but Mum was the best acrobat the circus had ever had. She died when the twins were born.'

He sat up, interested. 'Twins?'

Starre nodded. 'Misty and I and our brother, Prince, are triplets, and then there's Beauty and Storm, the twins.'

His eyes widened. The more he got to know these people the more fascinating they became. 'What about Blaze?'

'He's the oldest. We tease him and say he's just single. He hates that.'

'Your names. They're all …?'

Starre's eyes narrowed and he hesitated, realising she didn't appreciate the question. Misty, however, didn't seem to mind.

'Yes, the horses are all named after us.'

He let out a shout of laughter and even Starre looked like she wanted to smile. Misty looked puzzled before her eyes widened and she gave an impish grin. 'Okay, I mean we're named after horses. Dad's worked with heaps of horses over the years, so he picked our names.'

'What about your horses, then? What are their names if they're not Misty and Starre and Blaze?'

'There's Regal Zion, Dusty Lane, Montford Express, Steadfast Ever, and of course, Victorian Dream.' She glanced at Starre and her voice became quiet and strained. 'And Peter Pan. Or there was Peter Pan until …'

He watched in fascination as her eyelids began to droop and her face paled.

Starre glanced over and there was compassion and tenderness in her expression before she turned back to him. 'Peter Pan died of tetanus. That's how Blaze got sick. But I think we should head off to bed now.'

He sat up. 'No, not yet!'

Starre gave him a look. 'You can pay the consequences, then.'

'Consequences?'

'Once she's totally asleep, you can't wake her.'

He turned to Misty's semi-conscious form. She muttered something incomprehensible, then smiled.

'She smiles in her sleep?'

Starre stood. 'When she feels relaxed and safe. I think you're good for her.'

His face grew warm as he glanced at Starre then back to Misty. 'Should I wake her?'

'There's no waking her now.'

'But you can't just let her sleep there.'

Starre chuckled. 'No, what I can't do is move her. She's totally out to it.'

He raised one eyebrow. Anybody could be woken if you tried hard enough.

'Misty.' He called her name then came and shook her gently. There was no response. He tried again, calling louder. He even gave her a gentle pinch then looked helplessly to Starre.

'Are you sure she's alright? Is she conscious?'

'She's fine. She'll wake up fine in the morning. But for now your options are to leave her here for the night or carry her to bed.'

He was taken aback for a moment. She looked light enough, but … 'Would she let me?'

'She would let you do anything right now. I told you, she's out to it.'

The idea of carrying her appealed to him. Without another word he lifted the sleeping Misty into his arms, bending slightly under the burden.

'She's heavier than she looks.'

Starre grinned. 'You planning to tell her that when she's awake?'

He didn't answer but felt his face became warm at the thought. He doubted he'd ever tell her he'd held her so close. Starre held the cottage door open for him and watched as he lowered Misty onto her bed. Her eyelids didn't even flutter.

'You've got feelings for her, don't you?'

He jarred at Starre's quiet question but didn't immediately look away from Misty's sleeping form.

'I admit I've never met a girl like her before.' He made himself look at Starre. 'She's so, oh, I don't know …'

'Lovable?'

He grinned and tried to control the blush that filled his cheeks. 'Yeah, maybe.'

'She's different, Roy.'

She'd said that before, but this time he needed to know more. His eyes bored into hers. 'Tell me how.'

Starre sat down at the table and he followed suit.

'We nearly lost her when we were born.' Starre's dark eyes were searching his, as though trying to work out how much she could trust him. 'Dad told me once how she wasn't expected to live more than a few days. She was a weak baby and she didn't walk until she was two or talk until she was three.'

He shook his head. 'I don't understand. Look at her now! I saw her jump onto a wall and walk across it without stumbling. I've seen her on the back of that horse of hers.'

Starre nodded. 'Then I can guarantee that after she did those amazing things without even a stumble, she came straight home and slept. It takes every bit of strength and determination she has to do those things.'

'So what's wrong with her?'

Starre shrugged and leaned her chin in her hands. 'I don't know if there's anything wrong with her. Life is just a bit harder for her than it is for anyone else. She can't seem to do things naturally like the rest of us can. She has to think through everything, tell her brain to do the right thing, and then practise it until it becomes habit. Nothing comes naturally to her except her sense of humour and caring heart. But I wouldn't want her any other way.'

Roy nodded, his eyes catching and holding Starre's. 'Me either,' he said softly and he meant it.

***

Misty stood in the horse yard watching Starre inspect the horses and wondering why Roy wouldn't look her in the eye. She tried to remember what had happened last night. Had she said something to upset him? She couldn't even remember going to bed. Whatever had happened he was now making easy conversation with Starre but avoiding talking to her. She was sure she'd seen the hint of an awkward blush on his cheeks when he said good morning. Maybe talking to her took too much effort. He always seemed patient, waiting for her to make herself understood, and interested in what she had to say, but now she could see that it was so much easier and less stressful for him to chat with Starre.

Starre was being her usual, impressive self as she worked with the horses.

'Misty's doing a good job,' she called out. 'Constant Shadow will make an excellent performer.'

'Show horse,' Roy corrected with a laugh. 'We don't train horses for the circus here.'

Starre cast a look her way. She could tell Constant Shadow had been trained for more than showing. He'd been trained for the circus. She walked away before Starre could question her in front of Roy. She had to come up with an explanation and fast. It was too much to hope Starre would forget about it. She had to get to bed and pretend to be asleep so she could think. But she struggled to focus. All she could see was Starre and Roy standing there chatting comfortably, laughing and building a solid friendship. In some ways it was a relief to hear Starre's footsteps come to the door. She didn't bother pretending to be asleep.

'What's going on?' Starre sat on the end of her bed.

'I guess this sickness took it out of me.'

Starre shook her head. 'No, I mean with those horses you've trained for ring work.'

Misty was ready for it. Her eyes widened innocently. 'Oh, those. Mr Haydeen asked me to show him what I can do with training circus horses. He doesn't want Roy to know. He doesn't want to get Roy's hopes up but he's thinking they might make more money out of training some for performing as well.'

Starre smiled. 'Should we see if he wants to watch us all perform? Regal Zion's the best.'

'No! No! Mr Haydeen wants it to be a secret. He'll probably be upset that I even told you. Please don't mention it to him.'

Starre shrugged and let it go, though she still looked confused. Misty breathed a sigh of relief. She hated lying to Starre like that but what choice did she have?

Despite convincing herself she had no choice, she found herself in a bad mood all afternoon until Starre left to head back home. Trying to ignore her conscience was tiring work and made her irritable. Starre left early, saying she could tell Misty was tired.

Roy knocked on her door a few hours later and gave her a warm smile as he opened it and glanced around. 'Starre's gone home?'

Irritation rose up within her. He wasn't here to see her. He was here to see Starre.

'Yes, she went home.' She went to shut the door but he stepped in.

'And are you going okay? Feeling any better?'

She frowned. 'It's okay, Roy, you don't have to check on me. Like I said, Starre's gone.'

His brows rose before they narrowed again. 'What's that supposed to mean?'

'Just that I know you came here to see Starre, not me.'

He ran a hand through his hair, seeming agitated. 'That's not fair, Misty. And it's not true.'

'Everybody loves Starre,' she defended herself and accused him all at once.

He frowned. 'You think you can tell me who I love? You have no idea sometimes, Misty Clements.'

She glared back at him. 'I know what I'm like, Roy. I know people laugh behind my back or feel sorry for me. I know I'm not normal.'

She hated the tightness she felt in her throat and had to look away.

When he spoke his voice was deep and gentle. 'I might have laughed sometimes, Misty, but never behind your back.'

She looked back to see understanding in his eyes. He reached a hand to her shoulder but just as quickly let it drop. 'And I'm glad you're not normal. You're one of the most interesting, talented people I've ever met.'

She wished she could read the message in his eyes. She stood looking at him for several moments, not knowing what to say. He'd completely thrown her.

He finally stepped back. 'I actually wanted to know if you think you're up to coming to church in the morning.'

Humiliation washed over her. She had been over-sensitive and lashed out at him when he truly had come to see her. She bit her lip. 'I was hoping to come. If you're still happy to take me.'

His smile was hesitant, as though unsure if she was still upset with him. 'I'm happy to take you. I'll pick you up at nine.'

'Thank you.'

She watched him go, not knowing what she was thinking or feeling, apart from guilt. This man was the one she was going to betray. This was the man she was deceiving. It was all unsettling and confusing.

Chapter Fifteen

Misty searched through the clothes hanging in her wardrobe until she found a dress Starre had given her. Clothes were always so hard to match with their different colours and patterns, but with one single item of clothing, and one Starre had chosen, surely she couldn't go wrong?

'Ready, Misty?'

She came to the door and smiled at Roy. He was wearing the same clothes she had first seen him in that Sunday outside church. However, he was staring at her. She reached a self-conscious hand to her waist, then her hair. 'Is this okay?'

He smiled. 'Yes. I'm just used to seeing you in your work clothes, not so … so feminine.'

'Starre chose it.' She felt he had a right to know.

His smile deepened until it reached the corner of his eyes. 'She chose well. Ready to go?'

'I think so.'

She followed him out to his car, noticing the ground was a bit muddy. It must have rained in the night. She would just have to walk carefully, placing one foot in front of the other. If only she could wear her every day work boots. There were some disadvantages to wearing a dress.

Roy was getting ahead, walking in that sure but casual manner he had. She tried to speed up but knew the instant she did that it was a mistake. The ground beneath had become slippery. She managed to hold herself for a few seconds before the inevitable happened and she fell into the mud. A groan escaped as Roy turned. His eyes widened and then his mouth twitched as he drew in a deep breath. Then he laughed.

'It's all right for you to laugh!' She tried to shake some of the mud off her hands.

Roy simply laughed harder, while Misty began to pull herself up, studying the mud splattered across the bottom of her dress and all over her hands. She tried to glare at the still laughing Roy.

'I'm warning you!'

He raised his eyebrows, still grinning. 'What are you planning to do? Push me in the mud too?'

He looked like he didn't believe she would do such a thing and it was too much to resist. With reflexes like lightning, she jumped up and knocked his solid form off balance. He fell with a thud on one side and before he could react she wiped her muddy hands down his face and clean clothes. With a gasp, he tried to sit up but she held him down. She leaned across him and gave a teasing smile, her sparkling dark eyes triumphant. 'Now you can go to church looking like I usually do.'

She went to move back but he grabbed her hands. 'No you don't. I have mud all down my face, I don't see any on yours.'

She pulled a face at him and struggled to get away.

'It's no use, Misty. I'm ready for anything now. And you're going to get mud on your face.'

She struggled for all she was worth but he managed to wipe some down her face before releasing her. He sat grinning, watching as she moved out of his reach. His eyes never left hers and something stirred inside her. Before she could identify the feeling tiredness overwhelmed her. Her eyes began to droop. *Oh no, please God, not now!*

She forced her eyes open to see Roy right there, his face a

few centimetres from hers. 'You all right?'

She nodded through a tired, sad smile. 'Yeah, just worn out.'

'But you were so full of energy only a minute ago. What happened?'

'I don't know. It just happens. But I'm starting to feel better.'

'Will you be right to come to church?'

She looked up at him through glazed eyes. 'Yes. I'm not going to miss church!'

He studied her a moment longer, then held out his hand. 'You'll need a shower first and I'll need to change.'

She frowned as she took his hand and allowed him to pull her up. 'I don't know what to wear.'

'Wear your work clothes.'

'I can't do that. Everyone else gets all dressed up.'

'I won't be. I'll have to wear work clothes too. I only have one lot of Sunday dress.'

She felt relieved and guilty all at once. 'Sorry. I shouldn't have done that to you.'

He merely grinned. 'I don't mind. Now go and have a quick shower and I'll meet you out here in your work clothes in a few minutes.'

She smiled as she watched him race off to the house to have a shower. Could it be possible that Roy Haydeen liked her as much as she liked him?

Misty sat beside Roy in the back row of the church. She struggled to make sense of everything that was said and sung. The tiredness she felt was overwhelming but she tried to fight it as long as she could. Her greatest fear was the end of the service when strangers would come and ask all kinds of questions. She was far better at speaking in front of a crowd than one on one. If only she could stand at the front of the church and introduce herself so that there would be no need to meet anybody individually at the end.

***

Please God, let Misty understand this sermon. Even I don't understand some of the words. Roy stopped praying as a feeling of pressure came down on his shoulder. He turned to find Misty's dark head resting gently against him. Surprised, he shifted to try to see her face and then saw that she was asleep. Her breathing was deep and even, her eyes shut fast.

At least they were in the back row. She would be teased mercilessly if anyone else in the church knew she had fallen asleep during the sermon. But she slept so deeply and the service would only go for another fifteen minutes at the most. Then what? *God, what do I do now?*

It would take something drastic to wake her. He moved her, shook her, whispered in her ear and even tickled her, but nothing received any kind of response. The last song began and he knew this was his last chance. Feeling as though he had no other choice, he drove his knuckle hard into her arm. He had worried she might let out a yell and was glad for the music, but instead he received a confused, hurt look that made him swallow hard. Unable to help himself he put an arm around her and drew her close.

'Sorry, but you fell asleep,' he mouthed. Her dark eyes turned from hurt to horrified in the space of a few moments. She glanced around at the people standing in rows in front of her as they sang the last song and jumped to her feet.

He jumped up beside her. 'It's okay. Nobody else saw you.'

***

Misty was not comforted. She had fallen asleep on Roy's shoulder. What must he think of her? He always saw her at her worst.

'Church is not for me,' she decided as the service ended, chairs shuffled and people greeted one another and looked her way. She stayed close to Roy, feeling like a caged animal.

82

'Come on.' He took her hand. 'Let's get it over with.'

She allowed him to lead her to a group of young people. She felt secure and loved with his hand around hers. Everything would be okay.

A girl watched them approach, her smile wide and friendly. 'Hey Roy, is this the new employee you were telling us about?'

He nodded and she wondered at the shine in his eyes as he looked back to her. 'Misty, this is Katelyn. She leads our youth group.'

Katelyn grinned as her eyes connected with Roy's. 'I'll have you know I also lead the puppet ministry now. I've been told it was your idea so I have to make sure you're a part of it.'

His face brightened. 'So it's all happening, then?'

She nodded. 'Our first meeting is on Friday at seven. My place.' She then turned her attention to Misty. 'I was praying for your brother. I'm so glad to hear he's okay.' She turned back to Roy. 'Did you realise Blaze Clements is one of the school-leavers our church is supporting through Bible college? I've never taken much notice of their names before, but when you said Blaze, he sounded familiar. Anyway, he's one of them.'

Misty stared at Katelyn. She had no idea what she meant by supporting Blaze but presumed it must have something to do with helping him financially.

'It's good to have you as a part of our church,' Katelyn told her with genuine friendliness. 'There are too many guys and not enough girls around here.'

Roy gave Katelyn a good natured poke in the ribs. 'Isn't that the way you like it? Less competition?'

She grinned back at him. 'You know that's not it, Roy Haydeen!' She turned to Misty. 'Don't put up with any of his cheek. Keep him in his place!'

Misty merely smiled, not knowing what to make of the banter and longing to be back in bed and fast asleep. She managed to meet a few more people before her words became more jumbled and she asked Roy to take her home.

It had been hard and she hardly understood a word spoken during the service, but she had to admit there was something special about the people. They felt like family; the type of family she always wished she had.

They are your family now.

She smiled at God's voice in her heart and remembered Blaze's explanation about being hidden with Christ in God. With Christ as her representative, she was a child of God, just like every other believer in that church. *Thanks for my new family, God!*

She fell onto her bed in the cottage and the world faded out.

Chapter Sixteen

Misty held the phone closer to her ear as though it would help her understand the babble on the other end. She laughed. 'Slow down, Blaze. You're talking too fast!'

She heard a deep breath before he began again, slower this time. 'I'm trying to tell you I've found Bonnie. I thought I'd never see her again, even though I prayed and prayed. I have my first church assignment and you wouldn't believe it, but it's Bonnie's church.'

Now she was really confused. 'Bonnie Blake? Bonnie who was burned when Marcos set our stables on fire?'

'Yes, our Bonnie!'

'But what's she doing in a church? She's not a Christian.'

He laughed with complete abandonment and joy. 'Wasn't, Misty. She wasn't. But God is a God of miracles. Bonnie believes!'

She frowned. It wasn't possible. Was it?

'And she looks so good, Misty. She just has a few scars on her arms and hands but she's healed. God never gave up on her.'

The news was slowly sinking in and building up in her heart until she thought she would explode with joy. God had brought Bonnie to know him, and then brought Blaze and Bonnie back together. Did God care that much about everybody? Did he care that much for her?

***

Misty was pleased when Starre came to stay for the weekend, but she couldn't enjoy her sister's visit as much as she usually did. She found herself worrying when Roy went off to his first puppet ministry rehearsal on Friday evening instead of staying back at the house with her and Starre. Blaze finding Bonnie had got her thinking. God really did care about every detail, so he must also care about her feelings for Roy. Katelyn was attractive and got along too well with him. It bothered her.

Starre seemed to realise she was distracted and left her to herself. The evening passed way too slowly and she sat back in her kitchen chair, waiting for the sound of a car returning up the farm road. The minutes ticked by slowly and finally she stood and began pacing the room.

Starre looked up from the book she was reading. 'Just face it, Misty, you can't get that guy off your mind.'

She grinned sheepishly, knowing she wasn't hiding it very well.

'Why don't you do something about it?'

She frowned. 'Like what?'

'I don't know, tell him the truth, maybe. That you've got feelings for him and would like to take your relationship to a deeper level.'

She groaned. 'Starre, he's out tonight with this girl, Katelyn, and they get along really well.' Apart from that there was her deal with Marcos but she couldn't tell Starre about that. 'It's probably for the best, anyway.'

Starre looked hard at her. 'You're just scared. You're scared of a guy liking you.'

'I'm not! Roy is just not for me. It's complicated.'

'What's complicated about it? He likes you, you like him. What more is there?'

She refused to answer but felt heartsick. There was a lot more to it.

***

Roy arrived home to see the cottage light still on. He wanted to see Misty tonight. A whole evening spent with his ex-girlfriend had left him confused. He and Katelyn remained good friends and sometimes he wondered if he had let a good thing go. But he had always dreamed of something or someone more than his old childhood friend, Katelyn Renton. They seemed to think the same, have the same dreams and hopes and even the same gifts. This new puppet ministry and the way she took it on so wholeheartedly just confirmed that she longed to reach out to people the way he did and that she saw the same needs in the community that he did. Still, was it enough? Was he just dreaming to think there could be something or someone more for him?

Disappointment filled him when Starre answered the door. No doubt Misty was fast asleep.

'Roy! Misty's been wondering how your meeting went.'

'It went well.' He glanced around and smiled when he saw Misty sitting at the kitchen table. She gave him a tentative smile in return and red crept into her cheeks as she threw her sister a glare. What was that about? He stepped into the cottage.

'I wanted to ask you something. Katelyn reminded me we have church camp next month. Do you want to come? It'll be a great way to get to know people in the church. They're usually a lot of fun too.'

Panic passed over her face and he knew he'd have to make it more enticing. 'I was hoping you'd perform for them. I mean, I've told them all about you, and now they need to see to believe. We'd have to take Victorian Dream with us, but there's plenty of room for her to roam around the campsite and it's all fenced in. Some of the kids would love to have a ride on her too. We usually have a horse at our camps for some of the kids to ride … or be led around on, anyway.' He knew he was talking fast and made himself stop.

She smiled at him. 'Okay, okay, I'll come.'

He breathed a deep sigh of relief and grinned triumphantly. Then he turned to Starre. 'Do you want to come too?'

Starre shook her head but looked very satisfied. 'I'm not part of your church, and even if I was, no thanks. You two go and … well, just go.'

Chapter Seventeen

Once in the car and on her way to church camp, Misty wondered why on earth she had agreed to come. Sleeping in a room with strangers was a terrifying thought. And she only had work clothes to wear. She would be sure to stand out. What if she dropped food all over herself in front of everyone? Even having Victorian Dream there was not a comfort. What if something happened to her or if some child wandered too close behind her and got kicked? If Misty could, she would have jumped out of the car and headed back home.

'Stop worrying.'

She glanced over at Roy and stopped chewing her fingernail. It was easy for him to be relaxed.

'Look, there's Charlie.' He pointed as another vehicle overtook them. 'I'm glad he decided to come.'

Misty wasn't so sure she was glad. Charlie worked with the show horses, traveling a lot and working with her whenever he was home. He was always polite and respectful but she worried he might pick up that the horses were being trained for the circus.

'What are you thinking?'

She looked over at Roy. 'That I wish I was home.'

He put on a sinister laugh. 'Too late now.' Then he grinned. 'No, seriously, you'll be fine. It'll be fun.'

She wished she could believe him. She also wished she could relax but her heart was beating fast and she could feel herself sweating already. How could she survive a weekend like this without falling asleep in the middle of a talk and embarrassing herself completely?

Misty felt completely lost. She had missed the introduction session because she was busy settling Victorian Dream into her home for the weekend. There had to be a way to avoid walking into that large, noisy hall. She gazed out at the surrounding hills. If only she could be racing across them. Victorian Dream leaned against her and she smiled, soaking in the familiar, horsey smell.

'Not going in for the session?'

She started at the deep voice behind her. A stranger stood there, his eyes seeming to smile.

He glanced at Victorian Dream. 'You must be the circus girl who does amazing things with that horse.'

'You know about me?'

He went to Victorian Dream and ran a hand over the horse's side. 'Yeah. I work here, so it was me they asked about bringing this horse. Nice horse, by the way.'

Nice? Misty felt he had underrated Victorian Dream, but didn't comment.

'So you're not going in for the session?'

'No. What about you?' She found herself warming under his gaze and a familiar blankness came over her mind.

'I own the place. I don't have to.' He shrugged. 'Not that you have to either, but I think you're expected to be there.'

She just stared at him, hating the way she blushed and also hating the knowing smile on his lips. It was as though he knew there was something appealing about him and was using it to his full advantage.

'Come on.' He smiled invitingly as he held out his hand. 'I'll go in if you go in.'

She bit her lip. It might be easier not to go in alone, but she'd prefer not to go in at all. She looked to his offered hand, then found herself holding out her own despite the fact she knew so little about him. She didn't even know his name.

His smile widened as he took her hand firmly in his and led her toward the noise and hype of the hall.

The moment they entered, she wanted to run, but the stranger still held her hand. A getting to know you game was in play and each person was making two statements about themselves, one true and one false. The group had to work out which was false.

'I am thirty seven,' Charlie told the group, 'and I don't like mushrooms.'

'The first one. The first one!' the group yelled, while Charlie grinned triumphantly.

'Wrong! I am thirty seven. I really am.'

Misty had suspected he was older than he looked and chuckled at the shocked exclamations around her.

Katelyn was next. 'I have a phobia of spiders and when I was three, I drank a half empty can of beer I found on the street and then slept for twelve hours.' She looked to her parents and brother. 'You guys can't answer this!'

Misty noted the way the group were looked at each other, unable to guess which was the lie, while Katelyn's family grinned, refusing to give anything away.

Everyone except Roy ended up deciding she had a phobia of spiders. The majority ended up being right, and she looked at Roy in mock offence. 'How could you believe that of me? You who have known me my whole life!'

He grinned. 'That is why I believed it, Katelyn. I know you better than anyone here and I know what you're capable of.'

She let out a gasp and flew at him, pretending to tackle him. With a laugh he warded her off while the church watched on, amused. Misty, however, was not amused. There was something between those two. She turned to leave now that the stranger standing beside her had released her hand but he grabbed it again.

'Where do you think you're going?' he whispered. 'It's

almost your turn.'

She shook her head, eyes wide with panic. 'I can't think of anything.'

He chuckled warmly. 'Come on, you must have some secrets.'

Secrets. He was right, but she had one she could never reveal. How could she tell this group she was helping Marcos steal the Haydeens' horses? Suddenly that was all she could think of, and when all eyes in the church turned on her, she shrugged in defeat.

'I don't know,' she whispered. 'I can't think of anything.'

'Come on, have a go, Misty.'

That was Roy and she looked defiantly at him.

'I could come up with something for you.' His grin was playful and she shook her head, thinking of all the worst things in her nature he had come across.

'Go on, do it for her,' Katelyn urged.

Misty tried to beg him with her eyes not to do it but he didn't seem to notice. He grinned. 'Okay, she is a thief and she owns three cats.'

His eyes looked intently into hers. What was the message there? She paled and her legs felt as though they wouldn't hold her up. A thief? Did he know about Marcos?

'She owns three cats!' the group called out, but he was shaking his head. 'No, she stole my shirt off the fence.'

She glared at Roy, adrenaline making her angry. 'I didn't steal it. I borrowed it,' she said through gritted teeth, her jaw aching with tension.

'Ah, but you didn't return it. Doesn't that mean it was stolen?'

Katelyn chuckled and hit him on the arm. 'Get a grip, Roy. How about you tell us one of your secrets?'

'Yeah, Roy. Your turn,' another person called out, and the stranger beside Misty smiled at her. 'Lucky I missed out,' he whispered in her ear. 'I can't think of anything either.'

She smiled gratefully, glad the attention had finally turned from her. She slipped out of the room while she could, knowing she needed to go and lie down. The room she was supposed to be sleeping in was way too small. She would just find a quiet spot out in the paddock with Victorian Dream and enjoy the freedom of fresh air and wide, open spaces.

Chapter Eighteen

Misty heard a stranger calling her name. At the same time firm hands grasped her shoulders, gently shaking her. She managed to open her eyes.

'You okay?' The man she had met earlier was gazing at her, his face filled with concern. Glancing around, she realised she was still in the paddock with Victorian Dream by her side. She smiled up at him.

'Yeah, just tired.'

Relief filled his eyes. 'I couldn't wake you.'

She nodded, still smiling. 'I sleep pretty deeply.'

He studied her a moment, then held out his hand. 'My name is Colin.'

'Misty,' she said, though she knew he already knew. He was appraising her with a warm, friendly interest. It reminded her of the way Roy had looked at her until he became used to her. Now Roy had his Katelyn and it was probably just as well. She could arrange for Marcos to take the circus trained horses without feeling any emotional turmoil about it at all. Couldn't she?

The whole camp continued in a similar manner with Roy in the middle of any action that was taking place and Katelyn right there by his side. Misty spent most of her time outside. Colin often sought her out and tried to encourage her to join in whatever activity was in progress. She felt like a misfit. It was a feeling she was used to but one she had hoped would disappear once she became a part of the Christian family. She simply didn't belong anywhere; she was too different. She was also troubled by the small part of the talks she did hear; about loving others in the family of God, and doing to them as you would like them to do to you.

Marcos had once attempted to steal Victorian Dream and she had been devastated. So how could she do it to Roy and his family? The thought bothered her and she worked on excusing herself. It wasn't as though Constant Shadow was Roy's pet. Those horses were merely business to him – a part of his work to which he didn't really have any attachment.

The other thing bothering her was the poster on the dining room wall with the Ten Commandments written on it. 'Do not steal' seemed to jump out at her every time she glanced in that direction.

The only real highlight of the weekend was her chance to perform for the church. She enjoyed the amazed expressions on their faces and their words of admiration as she balanced on the horse's bare back. She built up her tricks until she did a back flip followed by a somersault. The crowd gasped when she lowered herself beneath Victorian Dream and came up the other side as the horse continued a steady canter. She ended by standing on her hands, then jumping nimbly to the ground.

Colin came to her side as soon as she finished the routine. 'You're amazing!'

She shook her head, looking in the direction of Katelyn and Roy. 'Not amazing,' she contradicted vaguely. 'Just practiced.'

For the first time that weekend Roy's attention was no longer on Katelyn. He was watching her and his expression was perplexed. She headed toward him but was stopped by the people vying for her attention. Admiration was nice, but why did she have to be extraordinary before anyone took any notice of her; before she could fit in?

Misty was quiet on the way home and Roy wished he could get her to talk. He didn't think she was tired; she sat erect in her seat. It was almost as though she was upset with him, but what had he done? He tried making a few friendly comments but only received a grunt in reply. Finally he could stand the awkward tension no longer and took his eyes from the road to look at her. He swerved and she gasped.

'Keep your eyes on the road!'

His chuckle resonated through the car. 'What's got into you?' She had never snapped at him like that before.

She pulled a face. 'Nothing.'

'Nothing,' he imitated in exactly the same tone, then shook his head. 'You've been in a funny mood all camp.'

Her voice became quiet and he had to lean closer to hear. 'Maybe you should have left me there and brought someone else home with you, then.'

If only he could stop and look at her. He needed to see the expression in her dark eyes to understand what was going on. 'Why would I do that?'

She shrugged. 'I don't know, I got the feeling you didn't really want me around at camp.'

Frustration rose up within him. He had hoped she understood how much he admired and respected her, but she obviously had no idea. She seemed so focused on her weaknesses she couldn't see her strengths. And every time he'd looked for her she was either with her horse or with that man who owned the camp centre.

'It works two ways, Misty. It's not like you were trying to spend time with me. You didn't even come near me. I presumed you were happy.'

She didn't respond but he could tell she was angry. Her whole body had become stiff with offence and she was deliberately looking away from him, out the window.

He had stayed up late each night at camp and he was tired. It frustrated him that he couldn't seem to get through to her no matter how hard he tried. And even Katelyn had expressed her concern about the way Misty would suddenly become tired and clumsy. She thought there was something seriously wrong. But how could he ever help her if she wouldn't be open with him?

'Come on, say what you're thinking.' He knew it was tiredness speaking, but was unable to help his irritated tone. 'Just say it.'

She spun back to face him. 'Say what? Thanks for all your support and for making me feel so at home? Thanks for pressuring me to come, then abandoning me?'

His eyes widened in shock and surprise at the sarcasm bitten into every word. She had never been anything but sweet before. He managed to recover. 'I didn't think you needed me. You and Colin seemed to be getting along just fine.'

She glared. 'If you taken any notice of me, he wouldn't have thought he needed to help me fit in.'

He made a deliberate effort to put aside his own offence and consider that she was hurting. He swallowed back his pride and anger. 'I'm sorry if you felt neglected,' he finally apologised, his eyes still on the road.

She let out a laugh. 'Don't be sorry. I don't need you, Roy, and it's good to find out what kind of person you really are.'

He felt the full force of the apology thrown back in his face. He pulled over to the side of the road and just looked at her. She kept her eyes glued out the window.

'Misty,' he pleaded but she didn't respond. He let out a slow breath, releasing his tension. He didn't know how to take her right now. He was meeting another side of her, one he didn't like very much. He sighed. 'I think we're both too tired for this discussion right now.'

She turned to meet his eyes and he saw all her defences drop as her eyes welled with tears. 'Why do you have to be so nice to me?'

'Why wouldn't I be?'

When she didn't answer he tried a question of his own. 'Why do you keep letting me close then pushing me away again?'

She looked down and a tear dripped down her cheek. 'Can we just go home?'

Roy didn't know what else to do. He put the car back into gear and watched as her head lolled onto the seat and she fell fast asleep. His father was right. Katelyn was right. Something was wrong with Misty Clements.

/ CHAPTER NINETEEN

Roy wanted to force Misty to go to a doctor. He wanted to insist she tell a specialist her life story and medical history. But she avoided him. She was polite but cool when he asked how the horses were going and told him she didn't need him to check up on her. She even accused him of not trusting her to do her job properly, so he left her alone. He didn't know what was going on. All he knew was that he felt the urge to pray for her often.

He had no idea what to say to her but he did know that God was asking him to pray for her. He needed to pray that her heart and eyes would be open to understanding Jesus' love. He'd prayed desperately for her brother Blaze's life all those months ago and now he felt as though he was praying for Misty's life; maybe her physical life, but more importantly, her spiritual life.

This whole walk with God is about life and death, he thought. *Eternal life and death. It's more important to pray for Misty now than it was to pray for Blaze. At least if Blaze had died he would have gone to be with God.*

***

Misty felt as though her heart was breaking and the only way she could bear the pain was to distance herself from Roy in any way she could. Constant Shadow was ready for Marcos and a heavy sadness came over her every time she looked at him. She had fallen in love with the horse. But even more than that, every time she looked at Constant Shadow she remembered Roy's kind, gentle face.

It was possible, she realised, that for the first time in her life she had grown to love a stranger more than a horse. She had also grown to trust a human more than an animal. In the middle of it all was her new-found knowledge of the one true God who had given everything, even his own life, for her. How could she throw it all back in his face by lying and stealing? Was it really worth it all?

Blaze had rung to tell her he and Bonnie were engaged. That was something she could never even dream about for herself. Because she was about to betray the one person in all the world she ever felt she could love.

I'm doing this because I love my family and want to protect them, Misty reminded herself each day as she watched Roy quietly work around her but never push himself forward. She knew he was respecting her need for space and was relieved, though she felt miserable. She missed him. Night meals became awkward and most conversation was directed between Mr and Mrs Haydeen.

She managed to avoid Roy until Thursday night when it was their turn to wash up after tea. She was aware of the way he studied her intently as she rattled the dishes in the sink. His eyes were still kind despite the way he no longer sought to spend time with her. She was aware that his usually cheerful face was sad. She had done that to him but she didn't know what to do about it. Tomorrow she planned to ring Marcos and let him know the horses were ready. She couldn't afford to feel anything for Roy Haydeen right now.

Crash! She jumped at the same time as the plate she was holding seemed to slip from her hand and to the floor. Flaming red, she bent to pick up the pieces but Roy was there first.

'It's okay, I've got it.' His voice was deep and reassuring.

She shook her head. It wasn't okay. Nothing was okay. He swept up the last of the chipped pieces with the broom and dustpan and emptied them into the bin. By now the washing up rack was full of the plates she had washed in the meantime. She tried to make it light-hearted and forced a cheeky grin. 'Can't keep up with me?' She pointed to the rack full of plates waiting to be dried.

He turned to look at her and his eyes were troubled. She threw her head away, scrubbing fiercely with the washing up brush and almost dropping the cutlery in her hands. She stopped short when his hand came to hers.

'What's going on, Misty? What's wrong?'

'Nothing I can tell you about.'

She continued washing, but his hand once again stopped hers. 'Then please tell someone. Tell God.'

She shook her head. 'I can't.'

The sadness in his eyes made her want to cry. 'Misty, God's children can tell him anything.'

She nodded. 'Maybe, but I don't think I can be a part of his family. I can't give God everything he wants from me. Not yet.'

***

Roy's chest tightened with a pain he had never felt before in his life. It was a love and concern deeper than romance; perhaps the kind of love and concern God felt for him, he realised.

'Misty, you don't understand –'

She cut him off. 'No, you don't understand. I can't be a Christian. There are too many rules and I can't keep them.'

'Rules?'

'Yeah, like the Ten Commandments and like that you have to not swear or smoke or whatever they are. I'm not used to rules. We didn't really have any when I was growing up, because nobody had the time or energy to make sure we kept them anyway.'

'I would have thought you had pretty strict rules for circus training.'

'Yeah, but not for anything else. It was easy enough to

concentrate for a certain time every day for practice sessions but I couldn't have done it all the time. Most of the time we were left to ourselves.'

He chuckled at her despite the heaviness in his heart. 'So basically you did whatever you wanted, whenever you wanted.'

She nodded. 'That's pretty much it.'

'So why aren't you a criminal now? Why didn't you kill your brothers and sisters if they upset you? Why didn't you fight for your own way, and fight to the death? Why didn't you lie and cheat and steal?'

She shrugged. 'Because I didn't want to hurt them, I guess. I love them too much.'

He smiled at her. 'That's how it is with me and God. I don't do things that will make him unhappy because it will hurt him too much and I love him. I'm not following rules all the time. I'm just living a life that makes him happy. I don't think God says not to smoke, anyway. It's just best not to because it wrecks your body and I don't want to wreck the body God gave me.'

She stared at him. If Roy spoke the truth, he spoke of a life that seemed possible. Perhaps God wouldn't expect more of her than she could give. And yet, Roy spoke of love. Could she love God more than her family whom she'd fought for her whole life? Could she refuse to give Marcos the horses and then sit back and watch her own family hurt? No, that was just too much to ask.

She looked down at the final saucepan she was washing. 'I can't be a Christian. Sorry. I just can't.'

The pain in his eyes was too much for Misty. She turned and left without even letting out the washing up water.

Chapter Twenty

Misty hated the thought of speaking to Marcos. She loathed the man. He was making her become just like him! She despised herself. Still, she forced herself to sit down at her kitchen table and begin a letter advising him the horses were ready. At least a letter was one sided. She wouldn't have to speak to him.

She jumped as a knock came at the door. Roy. He couldn't see the letter! She leaned forward, trying to cover it with her arms. But he was looking directly at it. Without even asking, he opened the screen door and walked in.

What's going on, Misty?'

He sat beside her, but his eyes were still on the paper beneath her arms.

'Nothing's going on. I'm just working.' She winced as she spoke. Now she was not only a thief, she was a liar too.

'On what?' He leaned forward, trying to see what she'd written.

She jumped up, her dark eyes full of fire. 'Mind your own business!' She turned the paper face down on the table.

Immediately she regretted her reaction, seeing the hurt and then suspicion pass through his expression.

'I think it is my business if it's to do with our horses. I saw Constant Shadow's name on there.'

She glared. 'What, am I not allowed to write a personal letter to someone and mention the horses I work with? You think I'm up to something? Don't you trust me?'

She couldn't look into his eyes any longer. They were too open. Too honest.

He rubbed the back of his neck then sighed. 'I don't know what to think Misty. I want to trust you, but you've been so … evasive. And I don't really know you. Not really. I can't work you out.'

She shrugged. 'Well, I guess that's just the way it is, then.'

He eyed her carefully before returning her shrug and heading toward the door.

'That's it?' she called after him. 'You're not going to force me to tell you what's going on?' She didn't know what made her say it. Perhaps somewhere deep inside she wished he would force her to admit what was going on and stop all the secrets and lies. She just wanted it to be over.

To her surprise, he spun around angrily. He opened his mouth as though about to say something, then shut it again, clenching his jaw.

She couldn't help provoking him further. 'I guess I'm not worth your effort. It's so much easier to spend your time on a normal girl without problems. That's fine. Leave me to my clumsy, confusing life. I've done okay on my own so far.'

She lashed out with words intended to sting but she didn't expect the reaction she got. He grasped her arms fiercely, holding her before him in iron grip.

'What about all the time I've taken to try to draw you out of yourself and stop you putting yourself down, hey? What about the hours I've spent cleaning up after your messes and the money I've spent buying new crockery? What about the way I defended you to Dad and offered to take the consequences if you end up being a liability to us? What about the times I've carried you to bed when you've fallen asleep in our house? What about all that, hey? Would I have done that if I didn't think you were worth the effort?'

She stared at him, aghast, her mouth open. Finally she closed it. 'You did all that?' she finally asked in a hoarse whisper. 'Why?'

His face came closer to hers, his eyes intense. His voice came out deep and soft. 'Because I fell for you the first time I saw you, that's why.'

He slowly bent his head, his mouth moving toward hers but she backed away, eyes wide. 'Don't do it, Roy,' she pleaded.

Hurt and surprise passed over his face. 'Why not?'

She couldn't look at him. How could she let him kiss her? She was about to use him and turn her back on all he believed and stood for. She was like Judas who betrayed Jesus. And here she was, looking into that face that had so struck her by its kindness. Tears filled her eyes as she turned away. 'I don't deserve your love! Please don't love me.'

His eyes retained tenderness and she saw that they sparkled with unshed tears. 'I wish I had a choice in it,' he whispered before leaving the cottage, the banging of the screen door echoing behind him.

Misty paced the room for several minutes, coming every now and then to the letter still face down on the table.

'What am I doing?' There was no way she could betray him now. There had to be another way. Carefully she stood on the kitchen chair and reached up to the shelf way above the stove. The tin she pulled down was heavy and full. Opening it, she stared down at the notes and coins it contained, then tipped it all out on the table and began counting. Years of working in the circus had built up quite an amount of money. She fingered the money she held in her hand. Her hands made it warm but she felt cold. She studied the face on one of the notes. Just a face, not anybody she knew and not anyone she could talk to.

'It's just plastic. It can get me anything I want, but it's just plastic.'

Suddenly she wasn't even sure what she wanted any more or what she had been saving for. A large house to live in alone and try to keep tidy? A nice car when she had nowhere to go? Any clothes she wanted when she didn't even have dress sense?

Maybe a new horse and the possibility of Marcos trying to steal it, or even worse, getting tetanus?

She knew in that moment, that when she died, she didn't want to be in a large, beautiful house with a magnificent horse by her side. No, she wanted to be surrounded by family and in that picture, she couldn't put aside the face of Roy. But most of all she wanted to be able to talk to God, to be sure she knew where she was going when she died. She wanted to be with Jesus forever. She had to talk to Roy. Now.

She ran to Roy the moment she saw him. He was working with Charlie.

'Roy, I need to buy Constant Shadow from you.' She tried to catch her breath. 'And some of your other horses too.'

She saw the look he gave Charlie. Charlie walked away, leaving them alone. He studied her. 'Buy them? You can have them as long as you're working here.'

She shook her head. 'No, you don't understand. I need to give them away.'

'To who?'

Her mouth went dry. She should have expected him to ask questions. There was no way he would just allow her to buy the horses without wondering why and where they were going.

'Please, Roy.' She held out her container of money.

His eyes widened as he looked in. 'Where'd you get all that?'

'Working in the circus. It's all honest money, I promise.'

He searched her eyes as though working out if he could trust her. 'No. Sorry Misty, I'm not letting you buy those horses.'

'But Roy, I trained them for …' She stopped short.

'I paid you to train them!' He looked so frustrated she imagined he would like to shake every secret out of her. But she couldn't give up that easily. She would just have to tell him.

'Roy, these horses are trained for the circus. I trained them for a purpose.'

Recognition began to dawn on his face. 'You trained them for yourself? To get money for yourself? To steal them?'

Her heart sank. 'No. It's not like that.'

'Then what is it like? Explain, because I don't understand.'

'I need these horses. Please, just take the money and let me have them.'

'I don't want your money!' He shoved the tin back toward her. 'What sort of person do you think I am?'

'Then what do you want?'

He shrugged. 'Something you can never give me now: a friendship I can depend on. Someone I can trust.'

Helpless tears of frustration began to fall. She had messed everything up as usual. Roy turned and walked away without looking back.

Oh God, I tried to do the right thing. I tried to fix it all up but I just can't. Now Roy doesn't trust me. I don't even trust myself!

'Trust me, then.'

She looked around, but knew the quiet voice had not come from a person. God was asking her to throw her life in his hands again. But completely, this time. Every last part of her. Including her family.

Please help me, God. I know I don't deserve it, but please sort out the mess I've made. You can have my life, because I can't do it anymore.

Her phone buzzed and she looked down. It was a brief message from Starre:

Just giving you the heads up. Marcos' Circus has just arrived here in town.

In Everdeen? The man was so brazen. He was so sure he would get away with whatever he did. She raised her eyes to heaven.

God, please help me here. I have no idea what to do.

Chapter Twenty One

It was with shaking hands and a heavy heart that Misty rode into the big top centred in the middle of the Everdeen show ground. Her continual prayer for help died on her lips as she gazed up at the magnificent tent flapping in the breeze. Memories were strong and she could almost hear the clapping and cheering, the sound of horses' hooves on the sawdust ring and the smell of animals. She pictured herself in her princess dress beside Starre, also a princess, and Prince dressed as a handsome prince. Then there was Beauty dressed as a fairy and Storm as Peter Pan. And there, leading them all, would be Blaze in his captain's outfit. All of them would ride around on their horses, impressing people with their appearance alone, before awing them with their spectacular performance on the magnificent horses.

She had loved and hated those performances. The adrenaline both excited and sickened her, the applause scaring and uplifting her at the same time. It was only the fact that she was there amidst her triplets and twin siblings, led by the fatherly Blaze, that kept her going. With them she had felt safe.

'Misty! I presume you're here with good news?' The deep, rough voice came from behind and she dismounted Victorian Dream.

She eyed Marcos carefully before answering. She had no idea what would happen today but she had left it in God's hands because there was nothing else she could do.

'I can't let you steal the Haydeens' horses, so I'm giving you Victorian Dream.' She blurted it out quickly before she could change her mind. She watched the man's red, round face, hating the hardness in his eyes. She shoved the tin of money into his hand. 'And this should cover the rest of the horses I can't give you.'

Marcos looked completely taken aback for a moment as he studied the money she held out to him, then his fixed smiled darkened into a frown.

'We had an arrangement, Miss Clements. People don't go back on arrangements made with me.'

She managed a cold glare despite her fear of the man. 'I have no choice. This is what I'm offering.'

'No, Missy, what you don't have a choice about is our arrangement.'

She narrowed her eyes and pushed the money back into his hands. 'I won't let you steal the Haydeens' horses, Marcos. If they disappear, I will know where they went.'

With that, she turned and walked away, leaving him staring after her. She couldn't look back. If she did she would run back to Victorian Dream, leap onto her back and ride her straight back home. There was a pain in her chest so intense she could hardly breathe. She needed to go and see Starre. However, as she headed toward her old home she realised she couldn't go there. How could she explain what she had done, why she was there without Victorian Dream? Instead she turned back the other way and headed toward the Haydeen farm. It was going to be a long walk home, but she refused to think of Victorian Dream any longer. She had done the right thing and despite the cost, it was worth it.

Hours later she limped in the Haydeens' gate, hot, tired and thirsty. Despite trying, she couldn't push Victorian Dream from her mind. Tears streamed down her face as she thought of life without her beloved horse. Her heart and head ached badly but despite her grief, one part of her felt relieved. She was through with lying and trying to take things into her own hands.

She limped into her cottage then jumped as a large hand came over her mouth. She felt herself spun around to face Marcos.

'What took you so long to get here?' His voice growled menacingly as he shoved her into a chair. 'How dare you try to threaten me and walk away from me like that?' He chuckled at the fear he saw in her eyes. 'I haven't finished with you or your family yet.'

He stepped behind her, his hand coming over her mouth again before she had a chance to scream. She longed to retaliate but he was strong. She had to stop struggling and just wait.

'Now here's the deal. I was never here, okay? You never saw or heard a thing. That was our original deal and that's the way it stays. But first, you are going to show me to the horses, just as an old friend. Show off the horses you have trained, then quietly walk away.' He leaned in closer, his eyes running up and down her body. 'Unless I decide to take you with me, of course.'

She drew in a deep breath. She had no idea what to do. He was so unpredictable.

Help me, God!

She knew God had heard her heart's cry and even the words she couldn't express for the hurt digging deep into her soul. She had laid her whole life, her inadequacies, fears, hurts and mistakes in God's hands. Despite still being trapped by the man who had made her life a misery, she knew complete peace for the first time. God would be her refuge. Where she failed, her God would succeed, and where she hurt, he would heal.

'Hidden with Christ in God,' she whispered.

Marcos stared coldly down at her. 'What?'

She didn't respond and he shook her roughly. 'Come on, show me where they are.'

She didn't know what else to do. She headed toward the horses, her mind working fast. Roy or Mr Haydeen were sure to be around somewhere. There had to be someone to help or witness what was happening. Where was everybody?

She had no idea when Marcos would be back with horse floats but she knew he would be. Nothing would stop him once he knew which horses he was after. And if he decided he wanted her too, she doubted anyone could stop him. She felt sick, knowing the man now had her money, her beloved Victorian Dream and would soon have the Haydeen horses, too.

He shoved her forward. 'So where's this Constant Shadow?'

She remained stubbornly silent, unable to bring herself to tell him.

'Show me!' He grabbed her wrist and twisted it until the skin burned.

Helplessly, she moved toward Constant Shadow. She needed to escape this awful man and all she could think to do right now was ride away on Constant Shadow and find help. It would be a big risk to take but it seemed to be the only way out. So, without warning, she came close to the horse, leapt onto his back, and with a shout, urged him toward the gate. It was shut fast, but she had always imagined this amazing creature could leap it if he really wanted to. She had never tried before, not wanting to injure him, but today it had to be done.

With speed that had her heart pounding, Constant Shadow jumped and she held her breath in those eternal seconds as they sailed over the gate. It was at the same time she heard Marcos yell out. She didn't even look behind. She had to get away.

The pounding in her ears drowned out all other sounds as she raced toward the open paddocks. Which way should she go for help? Into town?

Then she heard another sound and dread made her feel sick. Another horse's hooves were pounding the ground behind her, the angry rider shouting after her. Marcos could ride and it was possible he had come to the farm on horseback. That would explain why she didn't see a vehicle. He must have come ahead of her, passing her before she decided to head back this way. Now he was after her and gaining on her fast.

Help me God! She had to do something. Few people could ride like she could, and few horses were as fast as Constant Shadow. She slowed down deliberately, a plan forming in her mind. Everything within her wanted to gallop away as fast as she could, but she knew she had to outwit Marcos. Surprise had always been her best method of escape when she needed it and she needed it now.

The horse was very close. She leaned forward, ready to dig in her heels. She felt the presence of a man at her side and saw the strong arm that came out to grab the tether she had left on Constant Shadow. It was at that moment she chose to act. With a yell, she dug in her heels and Constant Shadow charged forward. At the same time she saw the hand around the tether twist horribly and heard the thud as a figure fell to the ground with a cry. It didn't sound like Marcos. She looked back.

What she saw made her cry out.

'Roy!' She brought Constant Shadow to a thundering halt and looked down to where he lay on the ground. She jumped down to his side, staring in horror at his broken wrist and the scrapes down his legs where his jeans had torn. He was looking up at her with eyes filled with pain and a coldness that froze her heart. He hated her at that moment.

'You're fired.' He spat the words out through gritted teeth and she knew he was in agony.

'Fair enough.' She was surprised how calm her words sounded when she was shaking so much. 'But let's talk about that later. I'm going to get help.'

He shook his head. 'No, stay here. There's a phone in my pocket.'

'Oh, good. I'll call the ambulance!'

His eyes narrowed. 'And the police.'

The police. Could they help? They had never helped before, but she had to trust Roy on this one. His eyes closed as she knelt beside him and took the phone from his pocket. With shaking hands she pressed the numbers he grated out, all the while listening for any sign of Marcos.

Once the ambulance was on its way she spoke to the police, pouring out the whole story and wishing she could control her trembling.

She watched Roy as she spoke and saw the way his eyes shot open at the mention of Marcos and the way he had treated her.

Tears burned her eyes as she gave the phone back to Roy. 'They're on their way.' She studied his face, once so kind and gentle and now contorted in agony. 'I thought you were Marcos coming after me. I'm sorry, Roy. I'm so, so sorry.'

'So am I. I thought you were stealing Constant Shadow. That's why I came after you. Why didn't you go to the police in the first place instead of doing all that scheming and lying?'

She shrugged. To be honest, she hadn't even considered it. The police hadn't helped her family in the past and she didn't expect them to help now. Circus people were used to being a law unto themselves. 'Do you think you'll ever be able to trust me?'

Anger flashed across his face. 'You didn't trust me, did you? You could have just told me what was going on months ago. Then none of this would have happened.'

She glanced back to his hand, feeling sick inside. It was clear he wouldn't be able to use it for a long time; the hand that had helped her with washing up, with training horses, with picking up the messes she made. It was the hand that was supposed to be bringing puppets to life in the park over the next few weeks of Christmas holidays. And he was holding his other hand at a strange angle as though it was paining him too. She had ruined everything.

Chapter Twenty Two

The ambulance officer looked at Misty. 'Are you coming too?'

Roy cut in through teeth still gritted in pain. 'No she's not.' His once kind eyes avoided her completely. 'She's going straight back to the farm to pack her things and go home. Her final payment will be deposited into her account.'

The ambulance officer looked between them and Misty tried not to cry. 'It's okay, I've told his parents and they're going to meet him at the hospital.'

The officer nodded, shut the door and drove away with Roy.

Misty watched feeling dejected and lost. What now? Constant Shadow and the horse Roy had ridden were grazing nearby. They needed to be taken back to the farm.

She could see flashing lights as she wandered wearily toward the house leading the horses. Then she saw Marcos and to her relief he was handcuffed and being led to a police wagon. But Victorian Dream was there too. She didn't understand. But then she saw the unfamiliar saddle on her back. Marcos must have saddled Victorian Dream and ridden her to the farm the moment she'd left the circus. Unable to help herself, she ran to her beloved friend and threw her arms around her neck. Victorian Dream nuzzled her gently, easing some of the pain that was eating away inside her.

Even though she had been indirectly involved in the attempted theft, she was not held responsible.

'You should have come to us the first time he approached you,' the officer taking Misty's statement said. 'There was an AVO taken out against him by your family a while back and we could have arrested him the moment he spoke to you.'

'AVO?' She didn't know what he was talking about.

'Apprehended Violence Order. According to my records it was taken out after he attempted to steal your family's horses last time. It means he wasn't allowed to approach or contact you.'

She stared. So all her turmoil, her stress and anguish had been unnecessary? She didn't need to protect her family. The police were already doing it.

'Sometimes you need to hand things over to those who are more capable of handling them,' the policeman told her gently.

She nodded in agreement. Like her life. Every part of it was better off in God's hands. Who other than her creator was capable of handling her life?

Emotion overwhelmed her as she rode out the Haydeen gate with all she could manage to carry. She would come back for her other items another day. She tried to focus on the fact that she had Victorian Dream with her and block out all other thoughts.

If only Blaze were here. She needed to speak with him. He always seemed to make sense, whatever he said, and right now she needed everything to make sense.

Normally, she was completely focused the moment she mounted a horse, but today her mind was too full. She was almost home when her eyes began to droop and familiar tiredness overwhelmed her.

No, not now! Jesus, help me, please ...

***

Blaze knew he had to go home. He didn't know why, but God's voice was clear. He was rounding the corner to the house when he caught a glimpse of something ahead. Some kind of animal was standing in the middle of the road. At first he thought it was a cow and slowed down. Then he realised it was larger than a cow. In fact, it looked like one of their horses. Victorian Dream! What was she doing standing in the middle of the road? And why was she just standing there? She was a smart horse and road wise. She had more sense than that!

It was only as Blaze screeched to a stop at the side of the road that he saw it. There beneath Victorian Dream lay a figure crumpled on the ground. With a cry, he leapt from the car and ran.

'Misty!'

She didn't move and he rushed directly to her, watching as Victorian Dream carefully stepped over her and to the side. The horse knew her owner would be okay now that Blaze was there.

He lifted his sister gently, knowing that first he needed to get her off the road. Once by the roadside, he shook her gently but urgently.

'Misty!'

To his relief, she was breathing, but fast asleep. He had seen her fall asleep in many places before but never while on a horse. Something must be bothering her terribly. But he wouldn't be able to get any answers until she had slept this off. He took her inside and lay her on the lounge. He studied her face lined with strain and the scar down her cheek. He remembered the day she got that scar; she had only been four years old and had fallen asleep after a performance. She had been sitting beside him behind the big top's curtain, on one of the props used for the trapeze artists. Then without warning she had fallen.

He had felt sick to the stomach as she let out a cry and stared up at him, blood streaming down her cheek. He wasn't sure what she had fallen on to cut her cheek so badly, but he always watched her closely after a performance from that day. She was wide awake and running on adrenaline throughout the performance, but afterwards she simply had nothing left to keep her going.

He had known it was Marcos who caused her stress that day. He had mercilessly ridiculed her for her clumsiness during practice and laughed at her when she tripped outside their caravan. He had told her she would never amount to anything, a claim Blaze had challenged angrily, causing Marcos to then turn on him too.

Studying her now, he knew Misty had been involved in a performance of some kind. Maybe not a circus performance but some kind of act that required her to be constantly alert and ready for anything. She had used up all her reserve and now she just needed to sleep.

Lord, what makes her this way?

Once he had just thought it was the way she was and nothing to be concerned about. However, this incident had changed his mind. Something had to be done.

***

Misty felt as though every muscle in her body had been drained. Now her strength was returning and she was aware that someone bent over her. She opened her eyes.

'Blaze! You're home. What are you doing here?'

He simply smiled and she stared around, hating the familiar confusion she was left with when she couldn't remember how or where she had fallen asleep.

'You fell asleep out in the middle of the road, Misty.'

She sat up, horrified. 'I what? On the road?'

He nodded and her eyes filled with tears. 'Why do I do that?' She sat up, desperate for answers. 'After every performance I always just needed to sleep. Now we don't perform any more but it still happens. Why is life so hard for me?'

Blaze gathered her in his arms while she continued to cry. She could hear him quietly praying for her and felt a security she had not felt for a long time. If God was like Blaze she knew she could trust him.

'Do you remember I taught you to walk?' He interrupted her thoughts.

She stared up at him, then shook her head at the quiet question.

'You used to get so frustrated because you couldn't keep up with Prince and Starre. You kept falling down and then you wouldn't even try anymore.' He reached an affectionate hand to her scarred cheek. 'So I took your hand and we practised until you were finally game to try on your own.'

She frowned. 'I thought we all learned to ride before we walked.'

He nodded 'We did. You didn't walk until you were two. You first rode a horse when you were eighteen months old.'

Her face fell. 'And Prince and Starre said they were eleven months.' She repeated what she had heard so many times.

'They did most things before you did but you have something that both of them have never had.'

She doubted it. 'What's that?'

'Determination and perseverance.'

She screwed up her nose at him.

'It's true, Misty. Nobody else I know works as hard at life as you do. You never give up.'

Discouraged, she shook her head. 'But it doesn't get me far, so what's it worth?'

'Respect. My deep respect.'

It was said so sincerely that she had to believe him and her heart lifted for a moment.

'You also have an ability to look outside yourself and care about others,' he added, then grinned. 'Normally, anyway.'

She frowned. 'That's only because I know other people are worth more than me. It's a waste of time spending my life on me.'

Even as she spoke the words, they hit her. It was true. Spending her life on herself was a waste of time, not because of her lack of ability but because of God. Whatever she did would never be quite good enough unless she did it for God. He was the only one who could help her and make her life worthwhile. Whether she had money, fame, respect or none of these, she would still die someday.

None of it would count on the day she breathed her last breath.

She was about to voice these thoughts when it all came rushing back. The memory of Roy lying on the ground, his wrist bent at a horrible angle. The coldness in his eyes as he told her to pack up and go home. 'Blaze, I've done something terrible.'

He smiled as though he didn't believe she could. If only he knew. Suddenly her words and thoughts were jumbled. 'I give, I gave Victorian Dream. I tried to give Marcos …'

There was silence for a few moments and she saw the shock in his eyes.

'Why would you do that? That horse saved your life today. She stood over you on the road until I got to you.' He took her hand and held it tight. 'Misty, don't give up – don't give up on life, on God, on yourself.'

'No, Blaze,' she tried again, tears of frustration now falling.

God, help me to speak. Please. I just want to tell him what happened. Please give me the words!

Blaze sat and held her hand while she pulled herself together. Then the whole story came pouring out. The threat from Marcos, her betrayal of Roy and his family, her frustration with her own body that would suddenly shut down.

To her surprise, Blaze didn't say a thing about her awful mistakes, her lying and deceiving. Instead he took her hand. 'Misty, you need to see a doctor.'

Her eyes widened. 'What for?'

'We need to find out why you fall asleep. A doctor might be able to help.'

'But circus people don't need doctors!'

He smiled. 'Once I thought that too. But if I'd taken you to a doctor a long time ago, you might not have suffered this long. You might not have risked your life today. God brought me home to show me the seriousness of your condition. We can't ignore it anymore.'

Chapter Twenty Three

Blaze thought she had some kind of condition? The thought both scared and relieved Misty. She never dreamed she could have something curable.

Blaze had to head home but first he made her a doctor's appointment. She would see the doctor the following afternoon, then she would ask Starre to take her back to the Haydeen farm to collect the rest of her belongings. What she would do from there she had no idea.

She shook as she apologised to Mr and Mrs Haydeen. They listened to her story without interrupting and with compassion and understanding.

'You're forgiven,' Mrs Haydeen assured her, 'and I'm sure Roy will forgive you in time.'

She shrugged. 'He has no reason to.'

At that, Mrs Haydeen smiled. 'I think he does. For a start, God has forgiven each of us, hasn't he? What right have we got to hold something against you that God doesn't even hold against you?'

She frowned, not sure she understood. For the first time since her arrival, Mr Haydeen spoke. 'God has forgiven everything you've done wrong. It cost him his life! If we refuse to forgive you, we're throwing that back in his face.'

She hadn't thought of it that way before. She gave a tentative smile, then accepted the hug they both offered. She dreaded asking the next question but she had to know. 'How is he?'

'The doctor says he'll recover completely in time. He has one broken wrist and the other is sprained. They operated on his broken wrist last night. Apart from a few other cuts and bruises he'll be fine.'

She closed her eyes at the memory of him lying on the ground in pain. If only she could turn back time. If only she had trusted him.

Mrs Haydeen walked with her to the cottage where Starre stood beside two packed bags. The rest of her belongings. She appreciated the look of understanding Starre gave her. She was having a hard time holding back emotion.

She was about to leave when Mrs Haydeen drew her into another warm hug, stepped back and looked into her eyes. 'If I had a daughter I would want her to be just like you.'

Her eyes welled with tears. 'But Mrs Haydeen, I wrecked your plates, I deceived you, I hurt your son.'

Mrs Haydeen shook her head. 'God used you to make Roy take his faith seriously and I've now seen him love someone, truly love someone, for the first time. And those plates? They're a small price to pay for your company each evening at the family table. I've grown fond of you, Misty, and I trust that in time you will be back.'

How could she respond to that? She tried to speak but felt her muscles begin to seize up. Not again.

'Misty?' She opened her eyes to look into Mrs Haydeen's, thankful she hadn't fallen. It had been brief this time.

'Misty, I think you should see a doctor.'

She smiled at the concerned Mrs Haydeen. 'It's okay. I did just before I came here. He wants me to see a neuro ... a neura ...'

'Neurologist?'

She nodded, surprised at the relief she saw in Mrs Haydeen's expression before she was swept up into another warm hug.

It was a bittersweet goodbye. Roy was angry with her, she had no job and she possibly had a serious medical condition but she had God. Hidden with Christ in God. His peace wrapped around her like a blanket and she knew that though she was hurting, everything was going to be all right.

Starre came with her to see the neurologist. Question after question was asked, then many tests were carried out. She had been terrified of doctors but now peace enveloped her as it never had before.

'Hidden with Christ in God,' she whispered over and over as she lay completely still, watching the medical equipment move over her, scanning her brain.

'There's nothing there God hasn't been aware of all along,' Blaze reminded her before the MRI, and she knew he was right. There was nothing to fear. Not even death. But still she felt sad.

That night she tossed and turned, unable to sleep. Every time she closed her eyes she would see Roy's kind eyes and the coldness that had come over them the last time he saw her. She remembered his broken, twisted wrist and the way he held the other one.

'Misty?'

She stopped at Starre's sleepy voice.

'What's wrong?'

She sat up. She had been unaware that her tossing and turning had been keeping Starre awake. 'Just thinking.'

'About the tests?'

'No.'

'About Roy?'

She didn't answer.

'You love him, don't you?'

She winced into the darkness then sighed. 'Yes, but there's nothing I can do about it. I wrecked his life.'

Starre chuckled tiredly. 'Come on, it's not that drastic.'

'It is. I stopped him being able to trust anyone. I made him love me, then threw it back in his face. I wrecked his wrists so he can't train horses for ages and he also can't be involved in the puppet ministry any more.'

Starre came to sit on her bed. 'So make it right,' she said simply, rubbing at her tired eyes and fighting for wakefulness.

She stared incredulously, then laughed. 'Of course, it's that simple,' she said sarcastically. 'Just make it right, hey?'

Starre smiled gently. 'That's right. There has to be a way. Find it.'

Misty had been revelling in her guilt for so long she hadn't even thought there could be a way to make things right. She thought God might perform some kind of miracle by using her life in another way but she had presumed her life with the Haydeens was over. Now Starre had planted a thought and God was beginning to make it grow.

It was true she had made a complete mess of things in the past when she tried to make them right but this time she would do it with God. She would depend on him for ideas, for help, for strength. She asked his forgiveness and felt peace. And then she asked him to direct her and show how her to make things right.

Chapter Twenty Four

Katelyn didn't know what to do. She had been to see Roy and it was clear he wouldn't be using his puppets for the Christmas show in the park. Without him, they were lost. There were always other people she could ask to fill in, but he was the one with the real gift and his puppet, Boomerang, was the one all the children came to see.

'Show me what to do, Lord,' she prayed, unwilling yet to give up on the ministry. God had given them the idea to carry out a program the week before Christmas so she had to believe he had a plan.

Suddenly she stopped and put down the puppet she held in her hands. The clip clop of a horse's hooves sounded down the street. Not even Roy ever rode a horse down the street of this town. She went to the window and watched in fascination as Misty Clements dismounted Victorian Dream. She came to the door.

'Misty. How are you?'

Misty looked awkward. 'I um … well, I need to tell you a few things.'

She opened the door to let her in. 'It's okay. I heard about the whole drama. No one holds anything against you.'

Misty gave a wry smile. 'Except Roy, but that's why I'm here.'

Katelyn was curious, but held off questions and invited her to sit down. She watched the way she sat then took one of the puppets in her hand. She turned it over a few times, then put her hand inside it. Suddenly it came to life, its every movement realistic, full of character and expression.

Her eyes met with Katelyn's. 'I ruined your ministry, and Roy's. I want to make it right.'

Katelyn was still watching the way the puppet looked around as though it were alive, though Misty didn't seem to be taking any notice of what she was doing.

'How?'

'I want to help with your puppet show.'

She tried not to look sceptical. 'You've worked with puppets before?'

Misty shook her head. 'No, but I know about performing and somehow I know this is something I can do. With God's help I can do it, anyway. I've thought and prayed about this and I just know.'

Katelyn stared at the puppet still moving in such a lifelike way on her hand. She suddenly moved it forward and close to her face.

'You doubting me, Katelyn?' the puppet asked in a gruff voice. 'You think I'm not up to this?'

She chuckled, but she was mesmerised. It was as though the puppet was someone different from Misty Clements. It had taken on a life of its own, a personality full of character and confidence. She had never seen a puppet speak so clearly through body language before. Even the voice Misty had given it was unique.

'You're a natural,' she agreed hesitantly, 'but what about the script? What about the whole show?'

It was there that Misty's face fell.

'Can we just do it as it comes? I mean, if we have a basic idea of what message we want to get across and then just go with it?'

She frowned. She wasn't good at working that way, but Roy …

'Misty, if we all work together I think we can do it.'

Misty looked puzzled. 'How do you mean?'

Excitement began to fill her as she saw how it could work. 'I mean, I will come behind the screen with you, just as backup to give you ideas what to say and stuff. I'm hopeless operating the puppets, but I always have ideas about what to say. Roy can do my job – he can be the person out the front having the conversation with you. He was so disappointed not to be involved, but this way he can be. And he's always trying to push me into throwing away the scripts and just letting the conversation happen. I can't do that but obviously you can!'

She stopped, her excitement disappearing when she saw the expression on Misty's face.

'I can't do it that way, Katelyn. Not with Roy. I mean, I thought I could just be behind the puppet theatre and no one would know who I was.'

Katelyn tried to understand. 'You don't want people to know who you are?'

'No. Especially not Roy. I don't think I could do it if people know who I am. That's the whole thing – I need no one to know it's me behind there. I need to hide or I will get all nervous and make a mess of it.'

Katelyn said nothing for a few minutes, wishing she could understand. Misty Clements was so different from anyone she had ever met.

'Okay,' she finally relented. 'I guess there's no need for anyone to know who you are. I'll just tell Roy we have a new puppeteer for him to work with. If he's willing to work with an anonymous puppeteer, then we'll do it. It could be difficult for you to keep your identity a secret, though; it's not like we have a secret entry in and out of the puppet theatre or anything.'

Misty grinned. 'I haven't had trouble escaping before. I'll do it again.'

She shook her head. 'I wish you'd let me tell Roy.'

'Please don't tell him. He will only be angry and he has a right to be.'

'Misty, if you think that, you don't know Roy. He's not the type to hold a grudge, especially against you.'

But she was insistent, and Katelyn felt excitement begin to build inside her. This really could work!

'Let's do it, then. I'll go and see Roy and we'll have a practice in the park early Saturday morning.'

Misty dimpled at her in delight and she knew why Roy had fallen for her. He needed someone like Misty Clements. *Please God, let them sort out their issues. Help Roy forgive.*

Chapter Twenty Five

Roy didn't know what to think. Here he was arriving at the park for a rehearsal with an anonymous puppeteer. The only thing he knew was the puppet's name was 'Tinsel' by choice of the puppeteer and that Katelyn was impressed with her.

'She's from out of town and she's a Christian,' she had said. 'She believes she was meant to come and see me and offer to help out with the puppets and by the timing of her arrival and because of her skill, I believe she is God's gift to us with our puppets this Christmas.'

He had to be content with that and to some extent, enjoyed the mystery surrounding the new puppeteer. It kept his mind off his own misery: his two painful hands, one useless for at least another three weeks, and his aching heart that couldn't quite forget a pair of dark eyes, a sweet, scarred face and intriguing personality.

Katelyn was waiting for him outside the puppet theatre and smiled warmly. His response was friendly but nothing more. He was itching to see this puppet.

'We finished making her last night.' She pointed to the theatre. 'Now, wait for it …'

He waited. First some hair and then two eyes peeked over the top of the stage. Every movement of the puppet showed an apprehension that was so real it made him want to assure it he was not going to hurt it. Suddenly, with a cute giggle, the puppet emerged completely and held out a hand for him to shake.

'I'm Tinsel. You must be Roy,' it said, and he smiled. He couldn't think of a better name for the puppet. Apart from the appropriate Christmas theme, the voice and sweet but cheeky character this puppet displayed made him think of tinsel. Even the voice was tinselly.

'It's brilliant!' He looked the puppet up and down, appreciating what he saw. The skillful hand behind it added even more personality to the carefully created character. He could have believed he was looking at a real, cheeky five year old full of energy and questions with a delightfully curious nature.

Katelyn smiled as she began explaining the basics of the message they were hoping to present.

'You're sure you're okay with ad libbing?' Roy asked, looking toward the puppet stage and Tinsel nodded at him.

'I've never done anything else,' she told him cheekily. 'Though that's because I was only made last night.'

He grinned, thinking he was going to have a lot of fun with this puppet. He was keen to get started.

***

Misty felt her heart beat faster when Roy first arrived in the park but there was something secure about hiding behind a dark screen and knowing you could see the people but they couldn't see you. Suddenly she felt the freedom and sense of achievement she'd always experienced as she cantered around the circus ring in front of the crowds. Being dressed as a princess had given her the freedom to be someone other than who she was. It allowed her to be one of the Clements performers, rather than Misty, the clumsy one. Nobody could see that behind her beautiful dress and princess crown was a lost, frightened young girl who might stumble at any moment. Even if she did, she was just 'one of the triplets'.

Here behind the puppets, she could falter or even be a fool, but it would be 'Tinsel' who suffered for it, never her. That gave her the freedom to take risks, and strangely, it was then that she didn't falter. It was then she was the best she could ever be.

If only I could live life like that. If only there was always someone to cover for me.

Even as she thought it, she knew there was. She could stand confident because every mistake she had ever made or ever would make was covered; hidden with Christ in God. And she was part of a bigger family, now. She was one of God's adopted children.

Katelyn stepped behind the screen and gave Misty's hand a squeeze. 'You ready for this?'

Roy stood out the front of the theatre as children and parents arrived in the park. He spoke with some of them, encouraging them to take a seat. He seemed to be enjoying himself.

'Yes, I think so.' Misty refused to think of herself and instead put herself into the character of Tinsel, the puppet who was about to meet a whole group of children for the first time.

'We have someone new for you to meet today,' Roy told the children, some who were chanting out the name of the puppet he usually presented. 'Boomerang's cousin has come to stay for a while, and she wants to meet you all. Do you want to meet her?'

The chanting stopped and the children immediately became curious. Then a game began between Roy and Tinsel. Roy would ask the puppet to come and introduce herself, but she wouldn't appear. As soon as his back was turned she would peek up over the edge of the stage and wave cheekily at the children. Roy pretended not to know what was going on and the children were thoroughly entertained, trying to tell him that Tinsel really was there. Finally he caught Tinsel in her game and introduced her properly. What followed was a conversation about Christmas.

'What is Christmas about?' Roy asked Tinsel.

She danced excitedly. 'Presents. And the Christmas man.'

'The Christmas man?'

'Santa.'

'What about the first real Christmas man?'

She looked around in confusion. 'Who was that?'

'I'll give you a clue – someone really famous.'

'You?'

He chuckled. 'No. He's also really strong and he knows everything.'

'Oh, it can't be you, then,' the puppet giggled, then put on a thoughtful expression. 'Is it the Prime Minister? The Queen? Um …'

'One last clue. This famous person knows you and loves you. He died for you.'

She grew quiet and Misty, behind the puppet, found her own heart constricting. For the first time, Christmas meant something to her. For the first time she truly accepted the gift offered to her by God; forgiveness through the gift of his son's life. The Son of God who covered for all her mistakes.

***

'It's Jesus,' Roy told Tinsel as something stirred in his heart. God gave him such a gift at Christmas. He sacrificed his own life, and yet he, Roy Haydeen, couldn't even give Misty Clements the gift of forgiveness. He shook his head. He couldn't be thinking about her right now. He had a puppet show to run.

The show continued as he tried to tell the story of the first Christmas when Jesus was born. Tinsel constantly interrupted with requests that he sing a Christmas song for them.

His lips twitched as he tried to ignore her crazy requests.

'Roy, sing the lullaby Mary sang for baby Jesus,' she pleaded. 'No, sing the baby song.'

Finally he turned, stopping mid-sentence and leaving his story telling for a moment. 'What baby song?'

'Baby Jesus in the old gum tree.'

His eyes widened and he gave in to his chuckle. 'Jesus was never in a gum tree. You probably mean the manger song. Jesus was put in a manger after he was born.'

'Oh, so was it baby Moses in the gum tree?'

'No, that was the kookaburra. That has nothing to do with Christmas.'

Tinsel looked disappointed. 'Oh. I thought that's why we have Christmas trees. I thought Jesus was born in a tree.'

Roy pretended to be frustrated. 'Well Tinsel, if you'd been listening to me tell the story instead of interrupting me all the time –'

'So was baby Moses the one in the wombat stew?'

He shook his head, still trying not to laugh at the outrageous questions this puppet was throwing at him. 'No, baby Moses was put in the river in a basket and God made a princess come and rescue him.'

'A princess?'

'Yes and Moses became her baby.'

'So God made Moses into a prince? Can he make me into a princess?'

Roy caught on and followed Tinsel's direction.

'That's right. Jesus came to earth so we could become princes and princesses too. He came so that he could take away all the wrong things we've done. That means we can become a part of God's family. And because God is the King of everything that makes us his children, princes and princesses.'

Tinsel leaned forward and spoke in a hushed whisper. 'So Christmas isn't just about presents?'

He laughed. 'Well, it is. It's about the biggest and best present there ever was. That's Jesus. God gave us Jesus and Jesus gave us his life so we can live forever with him.'

The children listened, spellbound, taking in everything Roy and the puppet said.

***

Misty watched Roy through the one way screen. He seemed to be enjoying himself as much as she was. But as soon as the show was over, she crept out the back of the theatre while he was still giving his finishing talk, and leapt over the park wall behind her. She raced to the grove of trees hiding Victorian Dream and rode home.

During the ride home her heart sang. She had never felt this way before. She believed the message she and Roy had just presented to the children and she knew she could now live it. She was truly that princess who had ridden around the ring on Victorian Dream for so many years and she was truly God's child. No mistake she had ever made was counted against her because it had been paid for by Jesus himself. She was completely safe and secure.

She let out a delighted laugh and wondered at the joy she felt. Tomorrow she would be back in that park, sharing the true meaning of Christmas with those children.

***

The show was over and the children and their parents began to disperse. Katelyn came to Roy. 'That was brilliant! You and Tinsel work so well together.'

He simply smiled as he moved toward the back of the puppet theatre.

'You were right. She has a gift. I'm wondering how many lines you fed to her, though.'

'Not one. She didn't need me behind there at all.'

He had suspected as much. He appreciated working with Katelyn but sometimes they simply weren't able to keep the same train of thought. This new puppeteer, however, seemed to know instinctively what he was thinking and how to bring out the points he was making. He also found it easy to follow the puppet's thoughts.

'You know Katelyn, as crazy as it sounds I feel like I could be closer friends with that puppet than with any real person.'

She chuckled. 'I'm sure you could, if Tinsel was a real person. I reckon maybe you could become close friends with the person behind Tinsel, though.'

Roy shrugged. 'Like that's going to happen when you won't even let me meet her.'

Katelyn smiled wider. 'I'm hoping you will meet her someday. She's a bit shy.'

He wondered about it. Tinsel seemed anything but shy. He knew what Katelyn meant, though. There were times he felt safer behind a puppet than he did in the real world. If Tinsel's puppeteer wanted to remain anonymous he would respect that … for as long as he could contain his curiosity, anyway.

Chapter Twenty Six

Misty arrived at the park early the next morning, surprised to see Roy already there. She kept out of sight, watching the way his eyes scanned the park.

She shook her head, both amused and irritated. He was looking for her. He wasn't going to make this easy.

She carefully leapt over the wall while he wasn't looking and crept into the puppet theatre. If only Katelyn would hurry up and make sure he didn't come to the rear. She waited nervously and kept a close eye on him. He wandered the park a few times, then finally came toward the puppet theatre. In desperation she threw her hand up so Tinsel appeared over the screen.

'Up to something, Roy?'

He jumped, then laughed. 'When did you get here?'

'I asked first.'

He looked flustered for a moment, then shrugged, looking distractedly past Tinsel to where Misty's head was hidden behind the dark screen.

'I don't know why you won't just meet me in person. I mean, you're talented – everyone was talking about you yesterday, asking who's the girl behind Tinsel. I felt pretty stupid saying I don't know.'

Tinsel moved directly in front of Roy's eyes so he couldn't focus so hard on the face he couldn't see behind the screen.

He pushed the puppet aside but she was insistent. 'You need

to learn to respect people's wishes, Roy,' the puppet told him, pushing herself back in his face, 'and I don't like the way you pushed me aside as though I'm just an object or old piece of material out of the ragbag or something.'

He laughed. 'That's exactly what you are.'

He turned as Katelyn arrived, and Misty sighed with relief.

'You didn't go in there, did you?' Katelyn demanded.

He looked sheepish. 'No.'

Misty produced Tinsel again. 'He was about to, though.'

Katelyn looked to him. 'Please don't, Roy. You could ruin everything. I can assure you that Tinsel will never perform the same way again if people find out who she is.'

He screwed up his nose. 'You know who she is.'

She ignored him and began updating him on the theme to present to the children for the day.

He looked impressed. 'It's excellent. Who thought that up?'

'Mmm …' Katelyn began, managing to catch herself as Misty produced Tinsel again.

'Me!' she said loudly.

He frowned. 'You can't have. You're just a puppet.'

She made the puppet glare with its body language. 'You're free to be more interested in the person behind me than you are in me but you don't have to be so obvious about it.'

He chuckled, though it was clear he was frustrated. 'This is crazy, talking to a puppet as though it's real.'

Katelyn grinned at him. 'You know that's what the best puppeteers do, Roy. Learn from it. Now let's get ready. Here come the children.'

'I'm so excited that it's Roy's birthday today,' Tinsel told the group of children who gathered around that morning. 'We can have presents and a cake, lots of junk food and a great big party!'

She danced around in excitement while Roy knocked gently on the imaginary door of the puppet theatre. 'Tinsel, can I come in?' His voice was soft and Tinsel continued talking.

'What do you want for Roy's birthday?' she asked the children. 'I want a doll's house. A really, really big one. And my brother's getting a game boy for Roy's birthday.'

'Tinsel?' Roy's voice was heard again amidst her chattering. She ignored him.

'My Aunty Hadberry is coming, and Uncle Huberto and all their kids. They might give me some presents for Roy's birthday too. I hope they get me good ones. They only gave me clothes last year. I want toys.'

Roy knocked louder on the door with his plastered hand and Tinsel sighed. 'Who's that interrupting?' She came to the imaginary door and opened it.

She shoved at him. 'Go away. We're trying to have Roy's party here. I've got lots of presents to unwrap.'

'But I'm Roy.'

Tinsel was already back to unwrapping presents, occasionally throwing the paper into Roy's face. She even tried to shove some in his mouth when he knocked gently again, much to the children's horror and delight. Eventually he called quietly until Tinsel came to the door and slammed it shut, hard. He pretended the force of it knocked him over and he fell backward to the ground as though dead. Tinsel didn't even notice. She was too busy with her presents.

The children laughed but the message got through.

'Is that how you treat Jesus on his birthday?' Roy asked the children as he got up from the ground. 'Do you just give presents to each other and have a big party and forget who it's really for? How about talking to Jesus this Christmas? How about thanking him for coming to Earth and giving his life for us? He wants to be friends with us. Let's not ignore him any more.'

Misty stalled as she listened to him speak to the children. There was something in his nature that captivated her. His eyes were kind, his expression so genuine. It hurt to know how badly her lack of trust had injured him. He still had a large plaster cast on one arm and a bandage on the other wrist.

She didn't have time to study him now. She had to escape before he came behind the screen.

***

Roy came into the theatre, expecting the puppeteer to have already disappeared the way she had yesterday. Instead he caught a glimpse of a figure retreating out the other side. She was so fast the glimpse didn't tell him anything he wanted to know. He gave in to temptation and went out to see where she went. To his frustration, he couldn't see her anywhere, and yet there was nowhere she could have gone in that space of time. There was a high wall in either direction and he was blocking any other escape.

As he glanced around, he remembered another figure who had also escaped in a seemingly impossible way. He remembered Misty Clements running along a high wall at the back of the church as nimble and stealthy as a cat. He shook his head, thinking how intriguing his life had become. There were certainly some fascinating people in this world. If only he could be attracted to people he could actually trust or whose faces he was at least allowed to see.

Chapter Twenty Seven

Roy watched Charlie work but he was restless. He itched to be able to work with the horses again but his hands were tied for at least another few weeks until they healed.

It was frustrating watching Charlie, because it just reminded him that Misty wasn't there. Charlie was nowhere near as good with the horses and Constant Shadow seemed to be pining for her.

He remembered her so vividly – the way she would stand eye to eye with the horses and speak calmly to them, her hands gently stroking their noses and necks. He longed to see her again but he couldn't give in to that longing.

He had to admit he wasn't angry with her any more; far from it. It was merely his need to protect himself from his own feelings that kept him from her. It was neither safe nor comfortable to have her working for him. He had never felt deeply for any girl before and the passion he felt now scared him. He was also confused by the growing attraction he had for the anonymous puppeteer he was working with.

What's happened to me, Lord? Everything feels so out of control.

Despite the unpredictability of all that was happening, he had to admit he enjoyed the air of mystery and excitement of the unknown. For so many years he had found life mundane but then Misty Clements had arrived.

She probably still thinks I'm angry with her.

It was true he had been hurt and disappointed at first but once he heard the full story of all she had been through his heart could not stay angry. In fact, his admiration, his respect and his longing to protect her had grown so strong it scared him.

He shook his head, knowing that letting her think he was angry was not being the Christian example Blaze had asked him to be. How could he show her Jesus if he had nothing to do with her? And she no longer had a job. That was his doing. He had fired her in a moment of hurt and anger before he knew the truth. Deep down he knew that whatever the cost, he still wanted to help Misty Clements.

Help me, Lord. I don't know what to do! Guide me as I talk to Misty. And help me know what to do about my feelings for her and the puppeteer.

Chapter Twenty Eight

Misty leaned Tinsel over the edge of the puppet theatre. 'Can we sing the song about Captain Underwear?'

Roy looked startled. 'What?'

The children gigged and Misty faced Tinsel toward Roy. 'What do you mean, what?'

'I mean what are you talking about, what are you thinking, what song could you possibly mean?'

Tinsel snorted. 'You're as bad as my heater with its hundreds of watts.'

Misty tried not to laugh at her own silly comment. Through the screen she could see Roy had that look on his face she loved; the one that would come when he wanted to smile but was holding it together.

He drew in a deep breath and pulled his mouth straight as he stood taller. 'What song are you talking about?'

She bounced Tinsel up and down. 'You know, bananas in pyjamas, and then the last line about Captain Underwear.'

He let out a snort. 'You mean *catch them unawares*? The words are *catch them unawares*.'

Misty knew they were going overtime, but the children were so enraptured Roy didn't seem to want to bring it to an end. He was looking toward the screen as though he wanted to rip it down. He turned back to the children.

'You know what, kids?'

She was tempted to throw in another smart comment about watts but let it go as the kids all chorused a 'what?' back to Roy.

'I've been wondering why Tinsel keeps hiding behind that silly puppet theatre. Do you think we should get her to come out here?'

The children all chorused an enthusiastic 'yes!'

Misty drew in a breath. Where was Roy heading with this? She tried to get Tinsel to speak but nothing came out. Roy was looking right at her despite not being able to see behind the screen, and his eyes were twinkling. She stood taller and straightened Tinsel at the same time. He was being too smart for his own good.

'So come on Tinsel, come out and meet the children properly. Or don't you trust us?'

She thought fast. 'Of course I trust you. I don't trust myself.'

His eyes widened. Clearly he hadn't expected that.

'You see, this puppet theatre is a bit like God.'

His brows shot higher and Misty held in a laugh. Tinsel had obviously thrown him this time. 'How?'

'Well, when someone accepts what Jesus has done for them, any mistakes they have made and will make are covered by him. They are perfectly safe. Hidden with Christ in God. When God looks at them, he doesn't see the one making the mistakes. He sees Jesus. Perfect Jesus.'

Roy frowned, looking genuinely perplexed. 'How is that like you?'

Tinsel leaned forward eagerly. 'Any mistake I make is blamed on the one in charge of me. And when I'm here, hidden behind the screen with my owner in control of everything, I am safe.'

His eyes lit up. 'I see. But then why can't you come out? If everything is covered, why can't you just be you?'

She smiled. 'When I try to do things on my own, without my owner, I make a mess of things. I couldn't come out without her.'

He grinned. 'So bring her out with you.'

Misty didn't know what to do. The truth was, she suspected she would do just as well without the screen to hide behind.

But to reveal herself to Roy now, in front of all these children, would not be fair to him. To her relief, Katelyn stepped in. 'Well, we've really gone overtime today! We'd better finish up. Say goodbye to Roy and Tinsel and we'll see you all tomorrow.'

She popped her head around the back of the theatre and Misty breathed a sigh of relief. 'Thank you!'

'No worries, but I don't know how long I can keep you hidden, Misty. He's pretty determined. I'm wondering if it's time you let him know the truth.'

She felt the blood drain from her face. 'I … I don't know if I can. Too much has happened. All he knows is the stupid things I did. I can never live those things down.'

Katelyn smiled. 'Just be yourself with him. Be the new person God has made you to be. You are amazing and beautiful inside and out and if Roy can't appreciate that he's not the one for you.'

***

Roy couldn't stand it any longer. He was desperate to discover Tinsel's true identity. He was about to race behind the screen when his father appeared from nowhere.

'Brilliant, Roy. Your mother and I were watching and we're impressed.'

'Thanks Dad, but there's something I've got to do.'

He moved toward the screen but his father caught his arm. 'I thought she wanted to remain anonymous.'

He shrugged. 'I know, but I have to know. Who is the girl behind Tinsel?'

Mr Haydeen grinned. 'Why?'

How could he answer that question? He wasn't about to admit he was falling for that girl. Her quick, witty responses, her wild sense of humour and reckless ways were appealing. Anyone with a mind and gift like that had his admiration. He didn't care what she looked like. He loved her personality. It had crossed his mind that she didn't want to be known because she considered herself unattractive. Maybe she was grossly overweight or had acne scars or was plain. He didn't care. He admired the personality he had come to know as Tinsel.

His father was grinning. 'I'm thinking you've got a severe case of Tinsellitis.'

Roy rolled his eyes and rushed away from his father. But by the time he came around the screen, Tinsel had gone. He sighed in frustration. He was going to see Misty Clements that afternoon and he had hoped to meet Tinsel before then. He couldn't have feelings for two girls and he needed to have that sorted before he saw her.

He didn't have any idea what he was going to say to Misty but he prayed that the right words would come at the right time. For a start, he knew he wanted her to work for him again, if only he could control his feelings for her. He would need to keep his distance; not that that would be a problem. She never needed supervision when she worked. He had only ever watched her work because he wanted to be near her.

His parents drove him home from the park as they had done since he broke his wrist. He leaned forward in the back seat.

'Dad, are you doing anything this afternoon?'

His father glanced at him in the rear vision mirror. 'No. Why?'

'I need to go and see Misty. I'm going to ask her to come back to work.'

A look passed between his parents in the front seat and they shared a slight smile. It annoyed him. He wasn't telling them this for their amusement. They obviously had no idea what this meant to him and what it could mean for his relationship with Misty. He wouldn't have even told them if he could drive himself but his damaged wrists prevented any secrecy.

'I can take you.' His father grinned. 'And I can make myself scarce for a few hours, too.' He looked to his wife. 'Got any shopping I can do?'

She chuckled. 'I'm sure I can invent some. Roy, how much

shopping would you like me to get him to do?'

They were laughing at him, he was sure of it. His eyes narrowed. 'Don't worry about it. I'll walk. Misty did.'

His mother sobered as she turned in her seat to look at him. 'Yes, and it took her several hours. Let Dad take you, Roy. We'll be praying for you.'

His Dad nodded, now serious. 'We will.'

He sighed in relief. 'Thank you.' He needed all the prayer he could get.

True to his word, his father dropped him off then drove away. He was surprised to find the Clements' home was modern brick with well-kept gardens. Knowing Misty, he had expected a run-down cottage with an unmown lawn and untidy surrounds. He admired the horses he could see in the paddock beside the house and smiled at the caravan with the remains of a campfire beside it. Obviously the family hadn't been able to give up their circus ways completely.

He knocked on the door, wishing his heart would slow down. It was Starre who answered.

'Roy!' She looked delighted to see him. 'I hoped you'd come to your senses.'

He attempted a frown. 'What is that supposed to mean? How do you know I'm not here to give Misty a hard time?'

She gave him a knowing smile. 'You're more readable than you think you are.' She shrugged. 'But you picked a bad time to come. She's out to it.'

Disappointment filled him. 'She's asleep?'

'Yep, and likely to be for a long time. She's had a busy morning.'

Dismay filled him. 'Doing what?' Did she already have another job?

'You'll have to ask her yourself. If she ever wakes.'

He ran his hands through his hair in frustration. 'Can I see her?'

She chuckled. 'Are you planning to try to wake her up?'

'I don't know. I just need to see her.'

She led him to the room she shared with Misty. He looked and saw Misty was indeed 'out to it', as Starre put it. She lay back on the pillow, her dark hair curling around her head and something close to a smile on her face. He looked to her hand and stopped short. Resting on her hand was Tinsel the puppet. Confusion washed over him at the same time as he heard Starre realise what he saw.

'Oh, no. I forgot she was practising.'

He spun to face Starre his mouth open in shock. 'Misty is the girl behind Tinsel?'

Even as he asked, everything fell into place: the way the puppeteer had disappeared so quickly, the way he felt about her despite having thought he'd never met her, and of course, the reason behind her desire to be anonymous. It all made sense now.

He moved closer to the bed, looking down at Misty. He'd missed her so badly it hurt. She began to stir and slowly those dark eyes opened and blinked a few times.

'Roy!' She swallowed hard as she stared at him. 'What are you doing here?'

He stared back. 'I was going to ask you what *you* are doing.'

She sat up, totally confused. 'I live here.'

He nodded. 'But what about her?'

She looked down to the puppet still resting on her hand and her whole face paled. 'I, um, I am not do I didn't tell you say, I …'

He chuckled gently. 'You're Tinsel but you didn't want me to know.'

She nodded in defeat. 'I'm sorry.' Tears welled in her eyes. 'I know you don't trust me.'

His bandaged hand on hers stopped her mid-sentence. 'It's not you I don't trust. It's me.'

At her confused look, he smiled and tried to explain. 'I am just not used to feeling this way about anyone.' Warmth crept into his cheeks at the confession. 'It was easier to have you out of the picture but a lot more painful too. I want you to come back and work for me again.'

Her eyes showed her disbelief. Shaking her head as if to wake herself, she groaned. 'But what about the puppets? We still have a show tomorrow.'

'And we'll do it.'

'But, but –'

'Yes, I know who you are now but we'll be okay. You are the most gifted puppeteer I have ever worked with and I have no doubt you can do it. Even if you mess up a few words, it will just make it more entertaining. There's nothing wrong with a few mistakes. Hidden with Christ in God, remember?'

He loved the way she stared up at him as though she couldn't believe he was there. She reached and put her arms around his neck, pulling his forehead down to meet hers. The tears in her eyes began to run down her cheeks and she tried to wipe them away.

'I'm sorry, Misty.' He pulled back slightly so he could look into her eyes. 'I'm sorry for everything I put you through.'

'I'm sorry, too.' She shook her head. 'It's me who made such a mess of things and now I'm such a mess.'

He grinned. 'A very likeable mess, though.' He picked Tinsel up with his bandaged hand. It seemed like all his problems were solved. The two girls he had feelings for ended up being the one person. How God must have been chuckling about the whole situation, just waiting for him to learn to trust and discover the truth.

He smiled. 'Any ideas for tomorrow's show?'

She swallowed hard and he knew it might take a while for her to feel completely comfortable with him.

He reached for her hand. 'I have an idea. How about we entertain the children with an amazing horse performance? And I will tell them a few stories. Maybe we'll be ready to work together with Tinsel again the day after.'

She let out a slow breath and smiled up at him. 'I'd love to. I thought I would never be able to ride her again.'

He nodded. 'You gave her up for me but God gave her back.' Then he grinned. 'Do you know my Dad accused me of having Tinsellitis?'

She let out a laugh and it was free and beautiful. It was a long time since he had heard her laugh. He planned to make her do it more often.

Chapter Twenty Nine

Misty was lost for words but joy welled up from somewhere deep within. Roy was giving her a warm, tender look.

'So can we go for a walk? See your horses or something?'

Just be yourself. She managed to nod. Starre was standing in the doorway, a knowing smile on her face. 'Can I come too?'

She pulled a face. 'You're not helping, Starre.'

Roy threw Starre a cheeky look and wave. 'In other words, no, you're not welcome.' He took her hand and led her out the door. She glanced shyly at him. He just smiled and his hand tightened.

'You want to see the horses?'

'If that's okay.'

She nodded and called to them. They began trotting over but he wasn't looking at them. He was gazing at her.

'So when did you learn to use puppets?'

'I didn't.' She gave him a timid smile. 'It just kind of came naturally.'

His look became intense. 'You're the most intriguing person I've ever met in my life. On one hand you are incompetent in everyday life, on the other you do things with ease that most people can't even hope to learn to do in a lifetime.'

She sighed reaching out a hand to pat the horses. 'I know.'

He came closer, stroking the horses much more absently than she did. 'You don't like being extraordinary?'

'I'm a misfit, Roy. Wherever I go, whatever I do, there is no one like me. It's a lonely way to live. I don't belong anywhere.'

'Except in God's family. You fit there perfectly.'

The words were spoken quietly and she smiled. 'Yes. Except in God's family.'

She enjoyed the way he quietly admired the family horses. Even more, she enjoyed the wonder and admiration in his eyes as he met Prince and Storm for the first time. Prince was visiting for the weekend, having a well-earned break from uni, and Storm had arrived home disgruntled as usual after a long day working on the roads.

'So you're the man in love with my clumsy sister.' Storm's comment was gruff.

She would have been dismayed if Roy hadn't turned tender eyes to her and smiled before looking back at Storm. 'Yes, I'm the man in love with your extraordinary sister. I've never met anyone more talented.'

Storm grinned. 'Well, here I am.'

He chuckled. 'Sorry, Storm. I'm sure you're impressive and all but are you a puppeteer?'

Storm shook his head.

'Have you ever given up your horse and all your savings for your family?'

Again Storm shook his head.

'Do you fight every day to keep going despite your body letting you down? Do you love God and try to live for him with everything you have –'

Storm put up a hand to stop him. 'Okay, okay.'

He merely chuckled but Misty knew she had to tell him about her doctor's visits. She had told his parents but what if they hadn't told him? What if he had no idea she might have a serious medical condition? She had had enough of keeping secrets.

But there was no chance. Roy was already discussing horses

with them all and they were completely absorbed, hanging off his every word as he told them about show horses. She listened along with them, enjoying the exchange. It wasn't easy to impress her siblings but Roy had managed to do it.

'Did you ride over?' Prince asked Roy as they headed toward the house.

Storm sneered at Prince and pointed to Roy's plastered and bandaged wrists. 'What do you think, clever boy?'

Prince laughed goodnaturedly. 'I guess not.'

Roy chuckled too. 'I would have liked to but my Dad had to drive me this time. I can't wait to get back behind the wheel myself!'

Prince's eyes took on a new light. 'Are you hanging round for long? Do you reckon you could give me a driving lesson? Dad said we can use the car if we find someone to teach us.'

'I reckon I could.' He turned to Misty. 'What about you? Want to learn?'

She laughed. 'Roy, you know what I'm like. Do you really trust me in a car?'

He leaned close and spoke softly into her ear. 'I would risk anything for you, Misty'.

She blushed at the grins she saw on the faces of her siblings. But then she realised she would have to tell him. She couldn't let him take her in a car without him first knowing the truth.

'Roy, I might have … I'm waiting on tests. I saw –'

'A neurosurgeon? I know. Mum and Dad told me.'

He looked completely non-plussed and a load rolled from her shoulders. He knew and he hadn't run away or avoided her. In fact, he'd done the opposite.

'I'll be right beside you.' His eyes were reassuring. 'If anything happens I will be right there. I know you, remember? I know exactly what you're like.'

She dimpled at him and watched as Prince jumped in the driver seat of the car. 'Come on you two, hurry up!'

Though Roy was unable to drive with his wrists the way they were, he was a good, patient instructor. Prince seemed to find the whole experience exhilarating while Misty sat in the back, hoping to gain knowledge in theory before putting it into practice. Roy could see her in the mirror on his sunshade and kept calling back with teasing comments.

'What are you looking so nervous about?' He grinned at her and she attempted to relax.

'Not worried about my driving, are you?' Prince asked, also looking at her through the rear vision mirror. The action caused him to swerve slightly and she let out a squeal.

'You're such a girl.' Prince laughed, returning his eyes to the road and focusing again. 'Just wait till it's your turn.'

'I don't think you'll want to be in the car when it's my turn.'

'Or on the road. Or the footpath,' Roy said.

'Or in the country,' Prince put in.

She pretended to take offence. 'Hey, come on.'

'Sorry, the town then,' Prince said and she screwed up her nose at him.

'Maybe the shire, at least,' Roy added.

Misty turned on him. 'Right, that's it, Roy. If you want to come and meet my family, then take sides with them against me ...'

'Hey, it wasn't just me! Prince was saying things too.'

'Yeah, but he's my brother. That's his job.'

'Really?' Prince's eyes lit up. 'I have permission to pick on you because I'm your brother?'

'No! You're not meant to be listening. You're meant to be focused on driving.'

Roy and Prince chuckled and Misty smiled. It was good to see Roy getting along so well with her triplet. It was important to her that he did.

When it was her turn to drive, Prince had no qualms about sitting in the back. He gave a carefree shrug. 'If you drive like you ride I trust you with my life.'

Roy turned in the front passenger seat to meet her eyes.

'Misty, all jokes aside, I'm convinced you can do it.'

He began to give instructions but she felt sick. Here she was sitting in a weapon. Vehicles killed more people each year than guns and right now she could be putting more than her own life at risk.

She started the engine as instructed but then slammed on the brakes as soon as the vehicle started to move.

'Good start,' Roy teased. 'We only need to do that seven thousand more times and we might make it out the other side of town by tomorrow morning.'

'I just don't feel in control. At least you can communicate with a horse. It has a personality.'

'No, that's what makes a horse even more dangerous than a car. A horse has a will. A car can only do what you tell it to.'

She was doubtful but she managed to start the engine again now that it had stalled.

'Now, rev the engine as hard as you can, spin the tyres and take off down there.' He pointed down the hill.

She turned to stare at him in disbelief. 'What?'

'Go on, do it!'

She shook her head in refusal.

He grinned at her. 'I can see what a terrible time this car is giving you. It's got control of you.'

She rolled her eyes but grinned along with him. 'Alright, alright, you've made your point.'

She glanced in the rear vision mirror and saw Prince also grinning, enjoying every minute of her lesson. At that moment, she wished it would never end. She wished Roy could always be beside her and that she could be this comfortable with him and God and the world.

When the lesson had finished, Roy pulled out his phone to call his dad to collect him. Misty stopped him with a hand on his arm. 'Wait.'

He turned to her questioningly.

'I think we should use Tinsel tomorrow. I think the puppets get the message across really well and I think we'll be okay.'

He smiled. 'I'm sure we will be but are you sure?'

She nodded and he gave her an impulsive hug. 'Let's do it.'

They sat in the lounge room, side by side as he came up with ideas for the show. Misty wasn't certain how they would work in practice. Performing was something she struggled to prepare for. It never seemed to come together until she was on stage or in front of an audience.

She savoured the feeling of having him sitting so close to her. Her eyes flew to his when he took her hand in his good one and rested it between them on the lounge. 'What do you think about Tinsel actually coming out from behind the screen so the audience can meet you?'

She attempted to answer, but her words came out jumbled. She looked down at the hand holding hers and tried again. It was easier to speak when he wasn't looking so intently into her eyes. 'I think it might ruin Tinsel for the children. I'm hoping we can use her again in the future.' She blushed and stumbled even as she said the words.

He smiled, let go of her hand and lifted her chin. 'Am I really that scary? What is it about being face to face with me that throws you so badly?'

She shrugged. 'Maybe I care too much what you think of me.'

He came closer until he was almost nose to nose with her. 'Well don't worry, I think highly of you; probably more highly than you realise.'

She looked into those kind eyes which now held added tenderness. This time she took his hand and held it. Everything would be okay now, even if she messed up.

<h1 align="center">Chapter Thirty</h1>

Misty wasn't sure what to expect. People were arriving and she could hear the usual questions about her identity. She loved that she didn't need to keep a secret from Roy any more. She could just be herself and Tinsel could be free to be herself too.

Words came easily and the audience responded well. She only stumbled once and it was such a funny mistake that the children all laughed, thinking it was deliberate. She saw the way Roy sent a reassuring smile in her direction and her heart slowed its beat again.

As soon as the show ended and people began to leave, he came directly behind the screen and smiled into her eyes. 'That went well.'

'It did.'

Katelyn came charging in. 'Roy! I told you not to come behind here.' She turned to Misty. 'I'm so sorry –' She stopped when she saw the smile that passed between them. 'You already know?'

'Found out yesterday.' Roy put his plastered arm around Katelyn. 'Stop stressing. It's all sorted out.'

Her eyes were questioning until he moved away from her and put his other arm around Misty.

He smiled into her eyes and Katelyn let out a laugh. 'Finally! You two, I thought you'd never get yourselves sorted!'

Sorted? Misty wasn't exactly sure where she and Roy stood but she decided to enjoy every moment while she could.

Mr and Mrs Haydeen smiled from ear to ear when Misty returned to work on the farm. They helped her move back into the cottage and added more furniture to make her feel at home. Roy stood watching, unable to help because of his injuries. When his parents went back to their garage to collect a sideboard they no longer used, Misty came to where he was leaning against the door frame.

'I'm sorry you have to just stand here watching.'

He grinned. 'I'm not. I don't mind watching you at all.'

A familiar blush filled her cheeks but she smiled. 'I mean I wish I could do something to help your wrists get better quicker.'

He moved his bandaged hand toward her. 'I've heard you can kiss injuries all better.'

She laughed. 'If I thought it would work I would do it.'

He raised his eyebrows. 'Since I was a little boy I've been told it works. You wouldn't question my mum, would you?'

She screwed her nose up at him. 'I wouldn't dare.'

'So?' He waited, grinning while she came closer, not really intending to put her mouth anywhere near the dirty bandage covering his wrist. She was almost there when she somehow tripped on nothing, the way only she seemed capable of doing, and fell hard against him. He had been leaning rather precariously against the door frame and slid down until he was sitting on the ground beside her. She went to apologise but he was laughing and his tender eyes were close to hers.

'Come closer,' he ordered gently.

She did but questioned why.

'Because I think I just bit my lip on the way down. I'd like you to kiss it better.'

Her face heated and she choked on a laugh.

'Please.' His eyes crinkled in the corners but she could tell he meant it. She had never kissed anyone before in her life and felt way out of her depth.

'I can't.' If only she could think straight with Roy looking at her the way he was.

'Why?' His question was soft.

'Because I've never had any practice.'

'I don't think anything could go wrong, Misty.' He smiled and she stayed perfectly still as he moved toward her. She concentrated on his kind eyes, knowing that if she looked anywhere else she might panic and run. She drew in a deep breath as his lips met hers. Despite being out of her comfort zone, she could feel his tenderness and longing and found herself responding to that. He rested his bandaged hand at the back of her neck and ran his fingers through her dark, tangled hair.

When he moved back, she gave a shaky laugh. 'Your lips musn't be too badly injured if you can kiss like that.'

He gazed back at her with a silly smile on his face, then moved away as his parents' voices came toward the cottage. Misty stood and moved to the kitchen. She didn't know where to look or stand; her mind and heart were overwhelmed. Absently, she ran a hand over her mouth to wipe away the feeling that remained. She had enjoyed being that close to Roy and had been affected by the intimacy of the kiss, but what if he was making the wrong choice falling for someone like her? Did he really know what he was in for? Doctors were sending her for further tests and there was no saying what they might find. She glanced toward him and saw that he was still watching her intently. He gave her a gentle smile, then turned to answer a question his father was asking of him.

Help me, God. Help me do what is right.

***

Misty had only been back at the Haydeen farm a few weeks when she asked Roy for some time off.

'I need to go into the city because Blaze is getting married.' Her eyes shone with the wonder of it. 'He's marrying Bonnie! Finally! I've been asked to be a bridesmaid.'

'Bonnie?' Roy could tell the woman must be someone special but couldn't recall having heard her name before.

'She was a friend of mine at school. She was in love with Blaze but she wasn't a Christian. Then she got badly burned in a fire at our stables. Her family left and we thought we'd never see her again. But she became a Christian and she was attending the first church Blaze was assigned after Bible college.'

He smiled. 'So God brought them together, hey?'

She nodded and he loved the way her eyes sparkled with life and her dimples ran deep in her cheeks. Then she looked thoughtful. 'We're riding into the church. I'm a bit scared of riding after what happened.'

He felt nervous about the idea too, but he wasn't going to let her know that.

Her dimples had faded. 'I guess we'll need to find another horse for Beauty, my sister, to ride on.'

'I thought you all had horses.'

'We did until Peter Pan got tetanus, then Montford Express, Beauty's horse, was killed in an accident. And Prince sold Regal Zion to get a motorbike. I don't know what he was thinking!'

She sounded so incensed that he couldn't help smiling. 'Maybe that he didn't want to risk losing his horse to tetanus or an accident too?'

She frowned as though the thought had never crossed her mind. Then she smiled up at him. 'I love how you always think of other people. You're always so kind and understanding!'

If only. But he knew God was working on him. He thought about what she had said. They needed another horse for the wedding and Misty had trained Constant Shadow exactly the same way she had trained her own horse. 'I'm just thinking … your sister who lost her horse in the accident, do you think she might like to ride on Constant Shadow?'

'I'm sure she would love to!' She hesitated. 'But we're still trying to work out how to get all the horses to the city.' Her eyes suddenly lit up and she grabbed his arm. 'I know! Roy, how would you feel about coming to the wedding? You could bring Constant Shadow and Victorian Dream in your trailer then look after the horses during the ceremony and reception.'

He grinned. 'So I'm invited but I'm confined to being stable boy, you mean?'

'Um, well, kind of.'

'Will you tear yourself away from the wedding to come out and visit the horses? Lots?'

'Yes.'

'Promise?'

'I promise.' She suddenly looked at his wrist still in plaster. He saw the question in her eyes.

'It will be off before then. But even if it wasn't, do you think I'd let a bit of plaster stop me coming?'

She looked into his eyes and smiled. 'No, I don't.'

So it was settled. Misty kept her promise and Roy enjoyed watching her ride into the church on Victorian Dream, her blue bridesmaid's dress sitting beautifully on her slender form and making her look more poised and mesmerising than ever. She flashed him a smile as she gracefully dismounted, handed him the reins and headed into the church.

He watched the bride – a young woman with burn scars on her hands and arms, but with shining blue eyes – as she walked into the church to meet Blaze. Something in his heart stirred. He would like to see Misty dressed like that one day. And he would like to be the one in the church waiting for her to arrive; waiting for her to become his wife.

Chapter Thirty One

Roy's wrist was becoming stronger and he struggled to resist doing more with his hands than he should. Misty caught him working with one of the unbroken horses and dimpled at him. 'I know you're sick of me asking but should you be doing that?'

He held up his hand. 'I'm not in plaster any more.'

'Yes, but the doctor said it will be weak for a while and you need to take it easy till you build up strength again.'

He screwed up his nose at her but stopped what he was doing. 'It's driving me crazy, you know.'

'I know.'

He reached for the tether again without thought, then realised what he was doing and dropped his hand. 'Do you realise how annoying it is to have two good hands that don't work properly?'

Her understanding smile warmed his heart. 'I know exactly what it's like. I have a body that often won't work properly.'

He came toward her. 'When will you get your test results back?'

'Any day now. They have a good idea what it could be but want to know for sure before they tell me.'

He understood her frustration. He was frustrated too. He dreaded what the news might be, but at the same time, he hoped and prayed there would be an answer, a cure or treatment to whatever made life so hard for her. He stood beside her as she took the tether of the horse and took over. She skilfully guided the horse in a circle around her, getting it used to her orders. Unable to resist, he reached out and put an arm around her waist.

'Should you be doing that?'

She looked delightfully cheeky and he laughed. 'It's my arm, not my wrist.'

'Maybe, but your wrist is attached to your arm.'

'True, but I'm attached to you, so that makes it okay.'

He leaned over and brushed his lips against her cheek. At that moment the horse realised its trainer was distracted and took advantage of the situation. It gave a tug on the rope and raced off down the paddock, pulling them both to the ground.

Misty let out a laugh and shook her head. 'Roy, you're too distracting!' She moved to put some distance between them.

However, he drew her back. 'Don't you dare say it,' he warned, seeing the way she looked in concern at his hand holding hers there so firmly.

'Should you ...' she began anyway, then stopped. 'You realise that if you ever choose a life with me I will probably always be doing this?'

His eyes twinkled at her. 'What? Holding my hand?'

'No, dragging you down with me when I fall or injuring you as much as I injure myself.'

He heard the despondency in her tone and turned her face to his. 'I don't care. Besides, have you noticed that every kiss we've shared is after something like this happens?'

She moaned. 'I have noticed. Roy, life with me won't be easy. Life is hard for me, it always has been. If you chose someone like Katelyn —'

He cut her off. 'I don't want it easy!' He linked his fingers between hers. 'I like adventure; to step out into the unknown. I don't want a relationship with someone so predictable I can almost guarantee what her next words will be. I don't want to sail along in life without any challenges and I definitely don't want to be kissing a woman who doesn't make my heart beat faster.

'I love the way you make me feel, Misty. I love the way you keep me on my toes. I love everything about you, especially that look that comes into your eyes when you're trying to understand something about God. It makes me wish I could see the world the way you see it.'

She shook her head. 'What if the doctors change that, though? What if I become predictable?'

'Then I'll take the easy ride for a while, hey?'

When she still looked concerned, he held her tighter in his arms. 'If you don't want me, I'll leave you alone, Misty, but if there's any chance you will share this life's journey with me I'll be, well, happy is too shallow a word to describe it. Life will hold an excitement for me that it never has before. I know I can't make you feel the same way about me, and I can't promise the easy life you're probably longing for, but I can promise my love and commitment and deep, unreserved respect whatever we go through. I can also promise I will walk as close to God as I know how to.'

She began to speak, a panicked look on her face, but what came out was a jumble of words. She struggled to free herself from his hand and stood. 'Roy, I –'

Without warning she fell, and this time he saw it. She didn't just fall. Her whole body went into a spasm. It was only a few seconds but he saw it and he felt sick.

'Roy, I'm tired.' She attempted to stand but he pulled her into his lap from where he sat there on the ground.

'What are you doing?' Her eyes were half closed, her words slurred.

'I think you should just sit here for a while.' He didn't want to scare her but neither did he want to risk her falling again. Now he knew without a doubt, tests or no tests, there was something seriously wrong with Misty Clements.

'Roy,' she said in a half-hearted protest but he stopped her words with a kiss on her smiling mouth, then just held her tight.

She laid a hand gently on his arms. Then she fell fast asleep.

He sat on the ground holding her for a long time, praying, watching the way her body occasionally went into spasms so brief it would not normally be noticed. That was the way Charlie found them.

'Charlie, I think we need an ambulance.'

Charlie didn't even ask. He pulled his phone straight out of his pocket.

By the time the ambulance arrived, Mr and Mrs Haydeen had joined the group gathered around them on the ground.

'I knew something wasn't right.' Mr Haydeen looked devastated. 'I should have done something earlier.'

Roy managed a half-hearted smile. 'What, like take her to the doctor? She's already been. She's waiting on test results.'

'I know,' Mr Haydeen shrugged, 'but I just wish …'

'I know.' Mrs Haydeen placed a gentle arm around her husband. 'We all wish, but all we can do is pray.'

Roy went in the ambulance. He wanted to be there when she woke. She would be confused and need reassurance. He needed reassurance too.

Doctors rushed around the hospital, attempting to wake her and attaching all kinds of instruments and medical equipment to her body.

'I know this looks drastic,' one of the doctors said, 'but it's just a part of the procedure. I don't believe her life is in any danger. We're just attempting to diagnose the problem.'

Roy nodded, reassured.

'We're going to do some blood tests and scans first. Then we may be able to do some other diagnostic testing.'

Roy's heart sank. 'Are you thinking a brain tumour?'

The doctor shook his head. 'Too early to say, but her previous tests indicate some type of epilepsy. Is there someone in her family you can contact? Someone who knows her medical history?'

He thought for a moment. He didn't think Misty's father would be much help and Blaze was on his honeymoon. Maybe he should try Starre?

***

Misty woke dazed and disoriented. When her eyes focused on Roy she reached a hand to him. He took it gently, trying to avoid the drip line coming from her arm. She tried to sit up. 'What's going on?'

'Hey, it's okay. You fell asleep.'

'I know.' Her eyes were wide, her breathing fast. 'I always do. Why am I here?'

He swallowed hard, not knowing how to explain.

'Roy,' she pleaded, and the panic in her voice tore at his heart.

'It's okay. They just wanted to do some more tests. They think you might have epilepsy.'

'What? Well, I don't. You can tell them I don't.'

'How do you know?'

'My grandmother had it, and well, she wasn't like me. She had fits all the time.'

His eyes widened. 'The doctors might want to know that. They were asking about your medical history.'

She lay back against the pillow, looking resigned and a little calmer. 'Did I have a fit?'

'Kind of. Your muscles went funny and when you were asleep it was like they would go all tense and then relax again.'

'Was it safe? Was I working with the horses when it happened?'

She didn't remember their last conversation? When he had poured his heart out to her? 'No, you were safe. I was with you. You don't remember?'

She smiled. 'No, but I'm glad you were with me.'

A doctor walked in. Behind him was Starre.

She rushed to Misty and threw her arms around her. 'I can't

believe I didn't think of epilepsy sooner. I'm so sorry Misty.'

She looked bewildered. 'But Starre, we're circus people. Even Grandma didn't need doctors for her epilepsy.'

Starre laughed. 'I wish it was true, but we're just as human as the next person. Without doctors Blaze would have died when he had tetanus. If Mum had gone to the hospital to have the twins, she might not have died.'

She looked hesitant until the doctor stepped forward with a friendly smile. 'We're not all that bad. We might even have some answers for you. I'm certain we will discover what causes your episodes of muscles weakness and lethargy. Mild seizures can be aggravated by stress and can be put down to a nervous system disorder. It may be something more serious but I don't think we need to worry about that until we rule out something simple like atonic seizures.'

* * *

The tests were frightening for Misty, especially as the mild spasms continued, but Roy stayed by her side.

She reached for his hand as they waited for the doctor to come and tell them the results. 'I wish it was all over.'

Roy nodded. 'I know. But the neurologist said they have a better chance of diagnosing you now they've seen the fits and monitored you during seizures.'

'But what if …' Her voice trailed off as a doctor strode into the room. A triumphant smile lit up his face.

'You have a form of epilepsy caused by an abnormality in your brain but with surgery and medication we believe we can fix it. We have you booked in for surgery tomorrow.'

'Tomorrow?'

'Yes. We can't afford to wait. Something has triggered these episodes so that they're becoming more severe and prolonged. We need to deal with it now.'

She drew in a deep breath. It was all happening so fast. If only Blaze was here, but he was on his honeymoon and there was no way she was going to tell him. In fact, she had made Starre promise she wouldn't let him know. She remembered what he had been saying as he lay delirious in hospital.

Hidden with Christ in God.

Before Roy left for the night he found a Bible in the hospital drawer and opened it to the words in Colossians 3 verse 3. She smiled gratefully. She could read the words as often as she needed to through the night.

'The church people are all praying for you too.' He held his phone out to her to show her the text messages. Her eyes filled with tears. She had God and she had her church family. Her life would change in the morning but she wasn't in this alone.

Chapter Thirty Two

It was brain surgery day. Misty could hardly believe it. She took a deep breath. It was almost time and despite wanting to trust God, the enormity of what was about to happen frightened her. Roy had gone out into the corridor to phone the church people and let them know she was about to be taken to theatre, while she lay there tortured by her own thoughts.

She never dreamed her life would end this way. It was so wrong. Why couldn't she die doing something heroic like saving somebody's life? Or at least doing something she loved? Why couldn't she have fallen from her horse during a performance? She wanted her life to count for something. She blew out a breath and glared at the monitor beside her bed. The steady pulsating as it measured her brain activity was annoying, but it meant she was still alive. Why couldn't she be normal?

Footsteps sounded down the hall and her heart beat faster. She recognised that stride. And that voice. And the concerned face that peered around the hospital curtain. Blaze had come! She threw herself over the side of the bed and flung her arms around him.

His deep chuckle rumbled in her ear. 'Are patients allowed to perform such acrobatic stunts?'

The fear threatening to overwhelm her rolled away and she felt the full force of the smile that filled her face. 'I don't know, but they can't stop me.'

'I'm sure they can't!' He grinned back before looking down at her cannula. The annoying tube had somehow wound its way around him.

He carefully removed it and her smile dissolved. 'Blaze, did they tell you why I'm here? That I'll probably never perform any kind of stunts again after this surgery? I might never ride a horse again.'

'Yes. Bonnie told me.'

His new wife. Her heart sank further and she lowered herself back onto the bed. 'You shouldn't be here. You should be with her. I don't want you to cut your honeymoon short because of me.'

His dark eyes softened. 'I know, but I had to be here. You're my sister. Bonnie understands.'

'She's not upset?'

'No. She's the one who made me come.'

'How did you know I'm here? Starre promised not to tell.'

He gave a sheepish grin. 'You made Starre promise not to tell me. So she told Bonnie instead.'

She should feel annoyed, but right now she could have hugged Starre. It was so good to have Blaze here. He was studying her as he settled himself into the chair beside her bed.

'I hope you don't mind. I thought you might throw me out, but Bonnie insisted I should come anyway. She said she has a lifetime with me so it doesn't matter if I take a few days to be with you.'

She dimpled at him, letting him know she wasn't upset. 'I think you couldn't have picked a better wife. But God did so much to get you two together. I don't want to come between you.'

He laughed. 'Don't you worry about that. Fire or storm or disease or conflict aren't enough to separate two people if God has planned for them to be together.'

He was right. It was a miracle that Blaze and Bonnie had found each other again after so many years and so much heartache. 'I still can't believe how God brought you two together. Who would have believed what God had planned all along?'

He nodded. 'I know. I thought she was going to die when she was caught in that burning stable. Then I thought I was going to die when I had tetanus.'

She caught her breath as the blood drained from her face. His arm came out to support her. 'Misty?'

'I'm scared, Blaze. But you both survived.'

His eyes widened, 'You think you're going to die?'

She shrugged but felt the sting of tears in her eyes and knew they had betrayed her. She was terrified. Her mother had died. Death was a reality. Everyone presumed her mother died giving birth to the twins, but what if her mother had the same condition she had? The specialist said it was hereditary and was triggered by stress. Her grandmother had it. It was possible her mother had it too. Certainly giving birth could be classed as stressful. Maybe giving birth had triggered it and killed her.

She looked up as Blaze laid a hand on her arm, carefully avoiding the cannula and tube. 'It's going to be okay, Misty. You have the best neurosurgeon in the country. But even if he wasn't the best, we have to remember Colossians 3:3.'

'I know.' She drew in another deep breath. 'Whatever happens it's going to be okay. Whether I live or die, God is with me and will never leave me alone.' She leaned back on the pillows and forced a smile.

He grinned. 'Yes, but I still don't think you're going to die. Not yet. I reckon God likes a good love story; that's part of the reason he spared my life and Bonnie's. And I think that young man waiting for you out in the corridor would like to be part of God's story for your life.'

She blushed as she fought her smile. Then a shadow filled her heart again, settling somewhere deep in her soul. 'Blaze, if I die, tell him I love him.'

His eyes darkened in pain. 'You're not going to die! You tell him!'

'You can't know that. I like your theory about God and love stories, but I don't really think we can depend on it.'

He looked sheepish again. 'Yeah, maybe not. It sounded good though, didn't it?'

'The doctor said brains are complex and he can't guarantee anything.'

Their conversation was cut off as a wardsman breezed into the room. 'Misty Clements?'

She nodded, thinking he was way too cheerful. Clearly he didn't know what was at stake today.

He placed two solid hands on the end of her bed. 'Your turn. Ready to go?'

Ready? She would never be ready. But then Blaze leaned over the bed and gave her a tight hug. 'Colossians 3:3, Misty. Whether you live or die, there's no need to be afraid. I'll be praying every step of the way.'

He was right, so why did she still feel afraid? She couldn't remember feeling fear like this before; apart from one time. As the bed was wheeled along the corridor and she caught her last glimpse of Blaze, her mind filled with memories of that day eighteen months ago; the day she almost lost her brother.

When she awoke she wondered at the clarity of her thoughts. It was almost as though she had been in a dream. Only this time she was watching her life through someone else's eyes. This time she remembered what had happened just before her fit. She remembered Roy's words of love and the way he had held her tenderly.

'He loves me!' She smiled wider. 'And God loves me and has spared my life!'

'Misty?' It was the surgeon.

She looked at him in question.

'It went amazingly well.' He pulled off the theatre cap he was still wearing. 'We accessed the exact place in your brain we needed to. We were able to use keyhole surgery. If only you had

had medical assessment when you were younger, you wouldn't have had to live with this for so long.'

Regret passed through her but just as quickly it turned to thankfulness. If she hadn't lived with this condition would she have recognised her need for God? Would she be the person she was today? Would she have ever sought employment on the Haydeen farm and met Roy? No, she didn't regret the difficult years. They were what God had used to shape her into who she was.

'Are you ready to see your family?' The surgeon nodded toward the door.

She smiled shyly. 'I am, but can I see Roy first?'

The surgeon smiled in return. 'The young man who's been pacing holes in the floor out there? I'll get him.'

Her heart beat faster as she heard Roy's eager footsteps. Never had she wanted to see someone more in her life.

'Misty?' His expression was hesitant as he came around the curtain. Her eyes took in every line of his face. Everything seemed so bright and clear. Joy filled her as she smiled.

'Roy, I remembered! I remember what you said before I had the fit. It's all so clear. Everything is so clear!'

He stared at her, as though trying to take it in, then with a cry of delight, he came and grasped her hand in his. He entwined her fingers within his own then gazed at her.

'I love you,' he said, and the kindness she had first recognised in his eyes turned into something deeper. There was tenderness and a depth that took her breath away.

'I love you too.' She attempted to sit up.

'Hey, are you meant to be doing that?' His eyes twinkled.

She leant up on her elbows. 'I don't know but how can I just lie here? I'm too excited. Life is better than I could ever have imagined.'

He laughed. 'You're not even up out of that bed yet. Heaven help us when you are!'

Her eyes softened. 'Yes, heaven helped us, Roy. God has given us so much. I don't want to ever try to live my life without him ever again.'

His hand tightened on hers. 'Me neither.'

***

It was only a week later that Misty Clements was living life as she never had before.

'I didn't know how amazing it would feel to not get so tired and have like a fog or mist over my brain all the time,' she said to Roy as he sat across from her on the tree stump in his shed. 'It's like the lights have suddenly gone on and I can see through the clouds that used to be there.'

He just smiled at her. Through her mind flashed the memory of the first time he'd found her in this shed. He'd suspected she was stealing his horses or equipment.

'What was I thinking?' She shook her head.

He gave her a questioning look.

'How could I have considered stealing from you?' She blushed even as she said it.

He grinned. 'Yeah, how could you?'

'Roy, don't make a joke of it. Imagine if I'd really gone ahead with it.'

His smile faded but the sparkle remained in his eyes. 'No, imagine if I had never met you.'

She watched as he put his hand into his jacket. He pulled out something then knelt down on one knee in front of her. Slowly he held out his hand and she saw that in his palm was a ring.

'Misty, we don't know the future. We don't know what God's got planned, but we are hidden with Christ in him. Like you said, our life together might not be easy, but I just want to share it with you.'

'You want to marry me?'

'I do.' He spoke with quiet determination.

She shrugged. 'Yeah, why not? I wouldn't know what to do with an easy life, anyway.'

'Why not?' He chuckled as he stood and pulled her up to

draw her into his arms. 'What about, yes Roy, I love you and can't bear to live without you?'

'That too.' She grinned while he pulled her closer and brushed his lips against hers. The kiss deepened but they were interrupted by Mr Haydeen charging into the shed.

They both turned to look at him. His face was glowing with excitement.

'Sorry to interrupt, but you know the three Burron kids that came to all your puppet shows in the park?'

They nodded, remembering the three children who had listened so intently to every word they spoke.

'Well their father just rang and asked what time church is on Sunday. He and his wife were there listening to all the shows too. They said they want to start coming to church and living for God the way we do.'

Misty and Roy looked to one another, their eyes speaking of the joy they felt.

'Another reason for us to work together in the future.' Roy squeezed her hand. 'I think God always intended for you and me to be a team, Misty Clements.'

She smiled at him, her dark eyes speaking of all the love she felt.

'I do too,' she whispered, then reached up with confidence to kiss him.

'Hey, did you notice that?' He pulled back to look into her eyes. 'We didn't fall over. You didn't knock me down.'

She grinned. 'Yeah. Boring, wasn't it?'

He threw back his head and laughed. 'Boring is not the way I would describe a kiss like that, Misty. If that's boring, you can bore me for the rest of my life and I won't complain.'

***

As Roy looked at her he remembered the first morning he'd seen her, the morning he'd sat outside the church, watching through the mist as she approached. It was a perfect picture of how his heart had been then. He went to church but he had never truly allowed his heart to be in it. He had been a Christian but never allowed all his knowledge of God to truly affect his life. Everything had been hazy and misty. He hadn't known how to love or give his heart completely to anyone or anything. His life had lacked passion and conviction.

Then you sent Misty. Thank you, God!

The mist of the morning had risen and the fullness of the day had arrived. They were going to live it with all their hearts. Forever.

ALSO BY JENNY GLAZEBROOK

Blaze in the Storm
Bonnie's world is happy and carefree until Blaze Clements and his horse-crazy family arrive from the circus. Is believing in God the only way to make sense of the tragedy that strikes?

Heart of Thunder
Beauty Clements hates her name – along with everything and everyone. What will it take to get through to her? Can God's love and forgiveness free her from her past?

Clouds of Prayer
Prince Clements captured Rachel's heart the moment he left the circus and rode into her school. But she is a minister's daughter and Prince has no time for God.

Clinging to Rainbows
Tori is running from her past and from the law. Disguising herself as Storm Clements seems to be the only answer to her survival. But what if Storm finds out?

Forgiving Sky
Sky Clements refuses to accept anything from the father who abandoned her as a baby. It will take a miracle to forgive him. But what if that miracle is just waiting to happen?

www.ingramcontent.com/pod-product-compliance
Lightning Source LLC
Chambersburg PA
CBHW020615120726
47905CB00003B/803